Vengeance Acts Up

A Wally Morris Mystery

Other books by Joani Ascher:

Vengeance Beyond Reason

Vengeance Tastes Sweet

Vengeance Cuts Loose

Vengeance On High

Vengeance Runs Cold

Vengeance Acts Up

•

Joani Ascher

Twelve Puppies Publishing

Twelve Puppies Publishing

Many thanks to Deborah Nolan and Kim Zito, the members of my writing group, who keep my stories making sense and save me from my flights of not-so-fancy. As always, I am grateful to my friends and my family, especially my husband, David, who can make anything happen.

Vengeance Acts Up

The Grosvenor Community Theatre Presents

ANYONE ELSE

By Xancie Valent

Directed by Lance Palmer

Produced by Darby and Nanette
Granger

Hillary Parker	The maid
Courtney Haven	Mrs. Lucinda Corbett
Casey Clark	Emily Corbett
Paul Clark	Terrence Peters
John Dewitt	The secretary/assistant
Jamal Rivers	Tom
Andy Schwartz	Paul
Doug Norton	Mr. Peters
Marcus Freeman	George
Julie Golding	Sous chef
Keisha Edwards	Baker
Jennifer Waters	Girl three
Louise Fisch	Understudy for Ms. Haven
Set Designer	Babbette Fay

Flowers courtesy of Blossoms

Act One--Drawing room of the Corbett mansion

Act Two--Restaurant

The Grosvenor Community Theater wishes to express our sincere appreciation to the Grosvenor Performing Arts Center for the use of its facility. Also, all our thanks to general manager, Harvey Floyd. Special thanks to Louise Fisch, without whose enthusiasm and assistance we could never have succeeded.

1

Prologue

A hush fell over the audience as the curtains parted, revealing a drawing room decorated in a 1930s style. Wally Morris knew it well, since she had worked on it for weeks, albeit reluctantly at first, as part of the set design team. But something was wrong. The furniture was in the wrong place, in fact, the wing chair was missing, and there was a big hole the size of a trap door in the middle of the floor.

Hillary Parker, dressed for her role as the French maid, came onstage for her opening line to a burst of applause. Before she could open her mouth, though, she spotted the hole in the floor. She looked around, as if uncertain what to do. Then her eyes widened and she screamed.

The missing chair was rising on its own, coming up through the hole in the floor. When the back cleared the stage, the audience on the left side of the theater could see why Hillary was in such distress. In the rising chair was Wade Fuller, and he wasn't just playing dead.

Chapter One

Four months earlier

"I can't wait to get inside that house," Louise Fisch said, pulling Wally Morris along in her wake. Louise had been unwilling to wait in the valet parking line so they had parked around the corner, after much searching for a space, and she was making up for lost time. Wally hurried to keep up with her long-legged best friend.

"Hello, Mrs. Morris," a voice said. Wally looked up and saw Rolly Sherman, who was dressed as a valet. He had been a former student of hers almost twenty years earlier when she was a long-term substitute at the high school, before she started teaching nursery school, and he held a special place in her heart. He held that place in the hearts of many of the people in Grosvenor, she knew, ever since he signed up for the army after a troubled high school career and served so bravely. Unfortunately, a serious head trauma after a car accident had left Rolly having to occasionally struggle with emotional problems.

That didn't seem to be a problem today. "Hi," Wally said. "I see you're one of the volunteers."

"Yes, Ma'am," he said. "Welcome to Grovewood. This is going to be one great party and it's for a very good cause." He smiled and went off to open the door for another car.

Louise was scurrying ahead of Wally, between and

3

around people, all dressed in their individual versions of "lawn party attire" as the invitations had specified. Louise's interpretation of the day's required apparel was an ankle-length white cotton sleeveless dress with buttons down the front, a trace of lace around the high neckline, with a wide, white, canvas belt at her waist. Her long red hair was under a white summer hat with a brim wider than she was.

Wally had nothing in her closet that was even close. She wore pale lavender peau de soie slacks and a lavender hand-painted silk blouse with pink and blue flowers reminiscent of Monet. Her chin-length, Sable Mist-colored hair was uncovered and she could feel the troublesome left side curling in the humidity of the afternoon.

While Wally had known Louise would be this excited, she hadn't considered the ramification on her own sandal-clad feet of trying to keep up with her friend. The pace was more suitable for athletic shoes. "The invitation said this is a lawn party," Wally said, when she caught up to Louise at the entrance to the grounds. "Do you really think they are going to let us inside the house?"

"Of course they are. The new owners spent two years renovating every square inch of their home. They want to show it off, believe me. Didn't you read the invitation to this fundraiser? There will be a tour."

"It will cost you five hundred dollars, I'll bet," said a man's voice. Wally turned to find Fred Naysayer, really Neimeyer, the town curmudgeon, standing beside her. She was surprised that he'd paid the one hundred dollars minimum required to buy a ticket. He hadn't exactly dressed for the occasion, though, unless baggy shorts, a stained t-shirt, and black socks with worn athletic shoes were now acceptable as lawn party attire. "You're all a bunch of jackasses," he shouted as the crowd gathered to wait for the opening of the gates. "This is another colossal waste of taxpayer dollars."

4

He continued to rant about the folly being perpetrated on the people of Grosvenor, New Jersey, Wally's home town, but at least he moved away from the gates. The kind escort of a security guard probably helped.

Louise was frowning. "He's totally wrong. The performing arts center is the best idea they've had in years. It'll bring a lot of money into the town, not to mention culture. We won't be one of those towns that rolls up its pavement by ten anymore."

Martha Knight waved to Louise and came over to talk. "It's going to be so exhilarating," she gushed. The flouncy flowered dress she was wearing fluttered around from all her excitement and suited her stage in life. A decade older than Wally and Louise, Martha was settling happily into her retirement from her job at one of the big New York accounting houses. "So many famous people will come to town. We'll be rubbing shoulders with movie stars. I love the theater."

Her more straight-laced elder sister, Belle Schultz, who wore a simple pastel pink suit, shook her head. "Who is going to want to come to Grosvenor when just one town over there is a theater, and one town the other way is the New Jersey Performing Arts Center?"

Luckily, the gates started to open and the surging crowd pushed the two women back before either Wally or Louise had to come up with an answer. Wally and Louise allowed the wave of people to carry them into the grounds. Once inside, they took a moment to get their bearings and take in the French chateau inspired house and grounds.

People milled all around, but attendants, wearing white, were there to keep them off the grass, out of the spectacularly landscaped flower beds, and out of the house, at least at present. Waiters and waitresses carrying champagne flutes and hors d'oeuvres circulated among them, and hugs and kisses flowed as people spotted their friends and long lost acquaintances.

"Wally, how are you?" asked an expensively dressed woman who swooped in for an air kiss so quickly that Wally didn't have a chance to see who it was. When she did get a chance to look at her, she couldn't remember her name.

Louise, as ever, had Wally's back. "How are you, Maggie?" she asked.

Right, Wally thought. Maggie Mattoon. It was odd for her to forget a name, and she was beginning to wonder if she was having a senior moment, when she remembered that she had never really known Maggie. She'd only been introduced once—by Louise. In any case, a reply was in order, so she smiled at Maggie and told her she was fine.

Maggie leaned close and asked, in a confidential manner, "Aren't you just the teensiest bit bored these days? Nothing has happened in almost a year."

"What do you mean?"

"You know," said Maggie. "No *excitement*."

Wally looked at Louise to see if she had a clue what the woman was talking about and saw her friend with her mouth wide open. "How could you ask such a thing?" Louise asked.

"I didn't mean . . . Of course I don't want anyone to be hurt. But Wally seems to just keep getting involved in murders."

"No more," Wally said. Besides, it wasn't strictly true that almost a year had passed since the last event. There had been a horrible occurrence during the winter. But maybe Maggie didn't count out-of-town murders.

It both irked and amazed Wally that she had developed a reputation as being some kind of amateur sleuth. Ever since a teenager was kidnapped a few years earlier, whenever anything wrong happened in the town of Grosvenor, New Jersey, people seemed to expect Wally to sort it out. While it was true that she had helped the police with a few problems over the years, she was certainly not

6

interested in looking for trouble. Yet some people always looked at her as if some big mystery must be right around the corner.

She changed the subject. "I think the new theater complex will bring a lot of excitement to town, don't you?""Huh?" Maggie seemed confused for a moment, then caught on. "Oh yes. It will. See you later."

Wally realized Louise was no longer standing beside her and turned to find her over in the tent, gobbling down canapés. Joining her, Wally chose something wrapped in phyllo dough from a passing tray. While she savored its taste, she glanced around. As small a town as Grosvenor was, there were still lots of folks here she'd never seen before as well as good friends she had known for years.

An octogenarian plus couple strolled by, arm in arm, causing heads to turn. He was wearing a blue blazer, straw hat, saddle shoes, and an ascot. She was wearing a black hat with long feathers that complimented her outfit perfectly. Darby and Nanette Granger were well known in town for their interest in the arts as well as for their wealth. They were sure to donate heavily to the new performing arts center.

"The speeches are starting," Louise said. "Let's get a good spot."

Wally stood near the front so that she would be able to see. Most people were taller than she was, especially Louise, and she hated listening to people speak while watching the backs of the people in front of her.

The operations manager, Kaylin Irish, wearing a navy business suit, made her way to the top of the porch steps. She moved to the center and turned to the crowd, waiting for the noise to die down. She was clearly uncomfortable in the spotlight, but Wally knew that was no reflection on her desire to do a great job.

Kaylin's opening remarks were short, acknowledged all the key people, and introduced Wade Fuller, the chairman of the board of governors. Wally and Louise exchanged glances. Both their husbands had spent far too many hours listening to Wade's self-aggrandizing plans for the arts center. This was his chance to shine, to make Grosvenor a destination town, something to be proud of and something that would bring more money to the local businesses, especially the restaurants. His own restaurant had been under renovation for months in anticipation of the town's renaissance.

Wade had been renovating himself in that same time. He'd taken off at least thirty pounds, Wally estimated, had veneers put onto his teeth and spent some time with a dermatologist, correcting what his teen-aged years had done. He'd erased the gray from his nearly black hair, seemed somehow taller than the five-and-a-half feet he had been, and dressed more prosperously. For this occasion he wore a pale gray linen suit and matching shirt, with a hot pink tie.

"In a few short months," Wade said, before he proceeded to bore the crowd nearly to death. Several minutes later, he finally got to the point of his remarks. "As you well know, ladies and gentlemen, this cannot happen without the support of the community. For this reason we are asking you, the cream of Grosvenor society, to contribute generously to make all our dreams come true. You will be receiving some wonderful gifts when you leave today as a token of our appreciation for your generosity."

He paused to let the crowd appreciate their good fortune before he asked for reciprocity. "I hope, no, the Township of Grosvenor Village hopes, you will give generously. Thank you."

"Finally," Louise said, watching Wade leave the porch and mingle into the crowd to accept their congratulations. "Now let's go see the house. I've wanted to get in here since we moved to town. I'd been planning to try to buy it the minute it came on the market. I still can't believe it changed hands while Norman and I were in Hawaii."

Louise's real estate career often allowed her a chance to get inside homes she admired, but she had missed this one. She had been miserable when she learned it had sold in less than an hour for one hundred thousand dollars over the asking price.

Wally allowed her to lead the way and the two of them took a good look around the rooms that were open to the public. Photos of the rooms as they originally existed were in each room for people to see, as well as pictures of the rooms in the run-down conditions of the intervening years, which provided proof of the remarkable restoration. Little modern surprises gave evidence that the new owners also had whimsy and humor.

When the party started to wind down, Wally and Louise made their way back to the gate. The people who had been serving earlier now stood with gift bags for each guest and wished everyone goodbye.

It was all so elegant and refined. Wally didn't even mind that all that was in the gift bag were two free tickets to the not yet built movie theater and a donor pledge form.

#

When Louise dropped Wally off at home, it was to a house full of people and animals. Debbie, Wally's younger daughter, was visiting with her husband, Elliot, and their yellow Labrador retriever puppy, Saffron. Sammy, Wally's black Lab, stoically tolerated the puppy chewing his ear as if it were a stick of gum. Rachel, Wally's dark-haired elder daughter, had also arrived with her red-headed husband, Adam, and two carrot topped children, Jodi and Charlie. They'd brought their own version of black and yellow labs; the lower maintenance, stuffed kind.

Nate had thoughtfully made reservations for dinner so that he and Wally wouldn't have to cook while celebrating Nate's birthday, especially since they'd both had busy afternoon plans. They would all come back home after dinner, though, because Wally had made Nate's favorite birthday cake.

"Mark called while you were out," Nate told Wally. "He sent greetings from London to everyone."

Wally looked into his blue-green eyes with a face that betrayed nothing and smiled. She'd had no doubts Mark would call, since she had sent him an e-mail reminder. As the youngest, and the one who was rarely home, this year studying at the London School of Economics, Mark often let family events go by unnoticed. Wally had left nothing to chance.

"Have you seen my sunglasses?" Nate asked Wally as everyone got ready to go.

"No."

"I know where they are, Grandma," six-year old Jodi said. "Saffron had them. I took them away from her and put them on the table in the hall."

Wally said a silent oops. Nate's glasses were new, prescription, and probably not puppy proof. She went to the table and took a look at them before he could get there. There was some damage, but it didn't look too bad, only a few chew marks on the right earpiece. When she showed them to Nate, he just shook his head.

"Thank you Jodi," he said. "You saved them." He turned to the puppy's parents. "It isn't so bad."

Debbie looked a bit guilty. "If you need to replace them," she said, pushing her blond hair behind her right ear, out of the puppy's reach, while she put Saffron into Sammy's old crate so she could be safe while the family was out, "just send me the bill."

"Don't worry about it. They're fine."

It took two cars, but eventually the Morris family got to the restaurant. It was the perfect one for children, very noisy with no serious foodies who would frown on a baby carrier up on the table. The food was good, plentiful, and there were enough choices that even the pickiest eaters could find something on the menu. The restaurant's lack of a liquor license didn't really matter to Wally or Nate, although they knew they could have brought a bottle of wine with them, as several other diners had.

Nate waved at Telly, the restaurant's handlebar mustachioed owner. The man finished talking to another customer and came right over.

"My good friends," he said, hugging Wally and shaking hands with Nate and Elliot. He made a big fuss over Debby and Rachel and the children. Jodi could only gaze in awe at the largest mustache she'd even seen.

"I see that Neon is closing," said Nate. The restaurant, the most recent incarnation of a long-time fixture in Grosvenor, under several other names, had fallen on hard times. No one had offered to buy it, although it had one of the few liquor licenses allotted in Grosvenor, according to the state-restricted mandate.

Telly smiled under his mustache. "Yes. I've submitted my bid for the license. It looks like I'll finally be able to put in a bar. It'll cost me, but I'll make it up quickly. And don't worry, I'm going to renovate so we can have a children's area too. This place will still be family friendly. Not like you-know-whose."

Wally knew. Telly was referring to Wade Fuller's restaurant. There the food was an experience, not just something tasty to fill a stomach. Bringing children was discouraged, not only by the management, but also the diners themselves. Though Wade Fuller didn't have a liquor license either, people brought expensive bottles of wine with them when they went to the restaurant. If they were drinking a white wine, an ice bucket stand was instantly set up beside their table to keep it chilled. Glasses were switched depending upon which type of wine they brought, as if the restaurant itself were serving the wine.

Telly's less pretentious restaurant had generic wine glasses only. "This is more our style," Nate said to the restaurant's owner. Wally nodded agreement.

He smiled his appreciation. "Enjoy," he said, before running off to greet someone else.

By the time they got home, replete with doggy bags and balloons that Alberto, their favorite busboy, blew up for the children, it was late. As Rachel and Debbie got the children into their pajamas for the ride home, Wally got the cake ready. Everyone sang happy birthday to Nate/Dad/Grandpa, Jodi helped Nate blow out the candles, and they all gobbled down the cake.

Finally, after hugs, kisses and some parting pats for the two dogs, Rachel and her family left. Debbie, Elliot, and Saffron departed a few minutes later. Wally finally had the birthday boy all to herself.

Chapter Two

A quick knock on Wally's screen door was followed by Louise strolling into the kitchen and sinking onto a chair. She briefly acknowledged Sammy whose wagging tail showed his excitement at seeing this visitor, then brushed her forehead with her sweat-band-covered wrist and put out her hand for the glass of water that Wally hastily poured.

"What happened?" Wally asked. "I expected you an hour ago, and I didn't expect to see you sweaty and out of breath."

"I walked here. That's what took so long. It's a lot farther than I thought."

It was slightly over a mile, if Wally had calculated correctly, so not very far away. Wally, who liked to take much longer walks, had never walked it, however. It was up one of the steepest streets in town, and mountain climbing was not her idea of fun. Then again, for Louise, it was all downhill. "I thought you were coming here so we could go walking together."

"I was."

Something was up, Wally thought. Louise wasn't the exercise type. She was the one who watched Wally do laps at the pool, and who only got exercise while playing tennis and wiping the court with Wally. "What's the occasion?"

Louise grinned. "My new exercise program. I've decided to get fit." She held out her glass for a refill.

"Would you like some iced tea instead?" Wally asked.

13

"Sure." Louise looked around. "Is Nate working late tonight?"

"Yes."

"He's been working late a lot of nights, hasn't he?"

Wally poured a glass of tea for each of them. "Yes."

Louise frowned. "I didn't see his car."

Nate's office, where he conducted both his investment business and the insurance business that had been his father's, was in an old barn behind the Morris home. Most of the time he had a very short commute to work.

"He's not in his office tonight," Wally said. "He's at a meeting."

"Which committee is it this time? It isn't the performing arts center or Norman would be there too."

"The synagogue planning committee," Wally said.

"Too bad," said Louise. "It's such a nice evening; it would have been nice for you two to take a walk together."

Wally shook her head in puzzlement. "I thought I was walking with you."

Louise put her glass down. "About that. I was actually wondering if you could drive me home. Walking downhill is one thing. I don't think I'm ready to walk back up."

"I'll get my keys," Wally said. It was after 8:20 anyway, almost sunset.

"Thanks."

Wally and Louise wound their way to the Fisches' house in the growing July twilight. The lights of New York City shone in the distance in between the stately houses on the hill.

"You know," said Louise, "since you have so much free time on your hands with Nate busy nearly every night, maybe you want to go along with me to the community theater tryouts."

"You're trying out to be in a play?"

"I'm thinking about it."

14

"What's come over you? First you start to exercise, then you decide to take up acting? What's next?"

Louise laughed. "It was the other way around. First I decided to be part of the play, then I decided I'd better get into shape. I'm bored."

Uh-oh, Wally thought. She'd seen Louise bored before. When it happened, Louise did one of three things: she redecorated, she bought a new house, or she took up some hobbies. Her husband, Norman, preferred the third option, since it usually cost the least. But Wally was often roped into Louise's projects and was left holding whatever bag it was that Louise had picked up.

"If it's all the same to you, I don't think I want to be involved," said Wally. "I'd rather not be in the spotlight, so to speak."

"Oh, I understand about that. I just thought maybe you'd like to be part of it. Sew costumes or paint sets or something."

"I don't think I'd be any good at either. Unless they want them finger painted or hot glued."

"Maybe you could work on programs," Louise said. "I'm sure we can find something you can do. Don't worry."

"I'm not worried," Wally reassured her as she pulled into Louise's driveway. "I'm not even interested. You'll have to tell me all about it, since I won't be participating."

"We'll see."

Wally wondered when her friend started harboring thespian thoughts. Did she crave the smell of greasepaint? Did actors still wear greasepaint? Whatever the answers to those questions were, Wally would have to be sure to be supportive, as long as it didn't drag her into getting involved, on the off-chance that Louise was serious.

"Thanks for the ride. I need a shower. So I'll call you when the tryouts are being held. We'll go together."

Wally didn't bother to protest again. She was

laughing too hard.

    #

Louise was persistent. Wally started getting worn down putting her off about the upcoming tryouts. As the July twentieth date for the tryouts drew closer, it occurred to Wally that maybe Louise just wanted her to go along for moral support. She was more than happy to comply. "Just don't expect me to sign up for anything. It's not going to happen."

"Okay," Louise said, looking relieved. "Thanks."

The following Monday evening, Louise picked up Wally in her Cadillac and they headed over toward the old Christian Science church, the home of the local amateur theater. "*Anyone Else*," Louise said. "That's what the play is called."

"When will it be on?"

"Just before the holidays," Louise said, referring to the series of holidays that began with the Jewish New Year. It was followed in quick succession by the Day of Atonement, the Harvest holiday and the celebrations of the reading of the end and beginning of the Torah. "Darby and Nanette Granger, the producers, were careful when they made the schedule. They are very excited about it and they wanted everyone to have a chance to come."

Wally was surprised when they pulled up in front of the senior citizens building where Nate's mother, Tillie, resided. Three elderly ladies, full of excitement and chattering away at each other, got into the back seat of Louise's car. To Wally's further surprise, Tillie was one of them.

"You're trying out for the play?" Wally asked her mother-in-law. "We all are," Biddy answered, on Tillie's behalf. "Thanks for picking us up, Louise. None of us likes to drive after dark."

Since it was July, it was hours until dark, which only served to remind Wally how long she was likely to be involved watching the tryouts. But with Tillie and her friends present, it couldn't help but be interesting.

Wally looked at Louise. "How did this all come about?"

Biddy, the smaller of Tillie's two companions, cut off Orli, who was trying to explain. Tillie, in between the two, put one hand on each of their knees. "I'll explain, girls. She's my daughter-in-law."

Wally could feel that old sensation of frustration she got whenever she dealt with Tillie and her friends. By herself Tillie was the picture of reason. Put the other people in her building into the room and Tillie got bossy. It did not diminish Wally's love for her, but it was perplexing.

"Go ahead then," said Orli, somewhat begrudgingly.

"Louise is selling a house belonging to one of our new tenants. She was dropping her off one day and mentioned the play. We want to be part of it."

"I'm going to take tickets," Biddy said. "Orli will be an usher."

"You don't know that," said Orli. "Maybe I will sell the tickets."

"You can take turns," said Tillie. "I'm going to work at the refreshment counter. It's a fundraiser for the amateur theater. You can bake for us, Wally. It's for a good cause."

The three of them started talking about what they could charge for brownies versus cookies. Wally briefly wondered what would happen to her if she jumped out of the car while it was moving. A smile at the corner of Louise's mouth only irritated her more.

"I am not baking," she said, under her breath. "And if you knew Tillie and her friends were coming, why did you drag me along? They can give you moral support."

"Not like my best friend."

"Make that former best friend." Wally was only half

17

kidding.

There was no time to escape, though, because they had arrived. Several other people had, too, and the back of the church-turned-theater was full of hopefuls of various ages.

At seven-thirty a man walked onto the stage. He wore all black, looking very New York City, with pasty, never-outside-in-daylight skin. His hair was bleached blond, with a lock falling over his forehead.

He took off his reading glasses and put his clip board aside. "Ladies and gentlemen," he intoned. "I am Lance Palmer. Thank you for coming. I see we have a lot of people to audition, so let's get organized."

Biddy looked like she was going to swoon. "I'm so excited," she gushed. "He's such a force."

"As long as he stays on the wagon," Orli whispered. "From what I heard."

After some shuffling, each group was given sheets of dialogue to rehearse. At eight, everyone was told to take a seat in house right and wait to be called.

"House right?" asked Biddy. "What is that?"

Louise pointed to the right side of the theater. "It is over there." She had a faraway look in her eyes. Wally began to wonder just how long Louise had been dreaming of being on stage.

People started to be called for their auditions by which character they wanted to play. One by one they were either told to be seated on the side or thanked and told to stay around for a possible alternate job. Several left, a few in tears, but most people were pretty easy going about it. They joined the group that Tillie was in, all looking over the potential openings in stage crew, etc.

Another name was called. Wally waited expectantly for the woman to go up onto the stage. The woman seemed not to have heard her name until Maggie Mattoon whistled for her to pay attention.

The entire room went silent.

"Who did that?" shouted Lance, his face redder than Wally would have thought possible, given his pale complexion.

Timidly, Maggie raised her hand.

Lance pointed at her. "You. Get out. Your services will not be needed."

A hum filled the audience as people asked each other what was going on. Wally looked at Louise, who said, "Never whistle in a theater," as if it were obvious.

The rumble of conversation continued as Maggie, red-faced, walked up the aisle and through the door. Wally was about to ask what Louise meant when she looked up at Lance, holding both his arms up in the air.

"Quiet!" he roared. He took a deep breath and looked as if he wanted something, but shook it off. After taking a long sip from his bottle of water, he signaled for the auditions to resume.

Louise, at Wally's side, clutched nervously at her page. "Calm down," Wally advised. "You won't be able to read it if it's scrunched up."

"I'm okay," Louise said, over and over. "I'm going to be fine. I'm really quite a good actress, you know. I was the star in fifth grade."

When the time came for her to be called she rose nervously and went to the center of the stage. She was about to start her lines, when a noise at the door caught everyone's attention.

"I'm here," Courtney Haven called out, creating a breeze as she swept down the aisle toward the stage. "I have arrived. I'm ready to get my script and choose my leading man."

There was a buzz among the crowd. Wally could hear a few people talking about the new arrival. They seemed impressed that this former soap opera star was walking among them. "She'll get that part," one of the women trying out for the lead said. "I don't know why I bothered to show up."

Lance Palmer got up from his seat in the third row and turned toward Courtney. "The time called for signing up was seven-thirty. You're too late."

There was a collective gasp.

"Don't be ridiculous," said Courtney. "This play has no credibility without me. I don't have to abide by your silly rules."

"Please sit down," the director said. "Wait your turn."

Courtney opened her mouth but looked around and seemed to decide better of it. She took a seat by herself on the side of the theater.

Wally looked at her. Courtney was showing signs of age. To Wally's knowledge, she hadn't appeared in anything in at least fifteen years. Maybe there was a reason. Lance Palmer certainly hadn't seemed happy to have a seasoned professional available, at least not this one.

"Please continue, Mrs. Fisch," said the director.

Wally soon forgot to wonder about Courtney as Louise's audition progressed. While she watched, she began to realize that Louise was good at acting.

The director seemed to agree. "Please fill out this form," he said. "Make sure all your contact information is included."

Louise practically floated off the stage. Tillie and her friends congratulated her before Wally could even get close.

"It doesn't mean I am going to get a part," Louise said. "I tried out for the lead, and we all know Courtney Haven will be getting that."

"You don't know," said Tillie. "It could happen."

Wally suspected Louise was right, but didn't want to spoil the mood. "Even if you don't get that part," she said, "maybe you'll get another one."

"I don't think so. There is only room for one middle-aged woman in the play."

That silenced everyone for a moment. But then Louise straightened up. "It doesn't matter. I'm proud of myself. I didn't think I'd have the courage to do it, but I did."

"We'll continue this in five minutes everyone," said Lance Palmer. "Those of you trying out for the role of Emily, you're next." He hurried up the aisle to stand beside Louise. "I just want to make sure you are really interested. I can't offer you the lead, that'll have to go to that—pseudo-diva." He shook his head and took Louise's hand. "Anyway, I need an understudy upon whom I can count. If, for any reason, there is an opening, I want it filled with someone who will give it her all."

Louise just stood there with her hand in Lance's. Wally didn't know where to look, since the whole thing was so awkward.

"O-okay," Louise said. "I promise."

While the auditions continued, Louise sank onto a seat. "Did what I think just happened really happen? Did Lance say I'd be understudying the lead?"

Wally could only nod.

Biddy and Orli were chattering on and on about how handsome Lance was until Tillie got them moving toward the door.

"Thanks for inviting me," Wally said to Louise. "I'm glad I came along with all of you. That was certainly something worth seeing."

Louise laughed. "Norman will never believe it."

Chapter Three

Norman Fisch was having a bad day. Wally could see that her good friend was nearing the end of his patience as soon as she came out of the early August heat into his pharmacy. While there were usually several pharmacists on duty, today he was alone. Even the counter help seemed to be missing. The phone was ringing and a long line of impatient looking customers stood waiting to be helped.

"Did you call Louise?" Wally asked, as she went around the counter and started to assist customers.

"She's on her way."

"Oh, that's good." Wally turned to the crowd. "Who's first?"

For the next ten minutes she gave people their orders and rang up their payments as best she could. The line had thinned considerably by the time Louise arrived. "Thanks for helping, Wally."

Norman gave a grateful nod. "I would have lost my mind if she hadn't shown up."

"I could stay for a while," Wally offered.

Louise's eyes lit up. "Could you? Then we can run my lines when there aren't any customers."

This was the third time in a week that Louise had asked Wally to run lines with her. Wally hadn't minded, since Nate was spending so much time going to meetings lately, but she wondered if it wasn't a waste of time. When Louise wasn't running her lines she was telling Wally every detail of what was going on behind the scenes. To

Wally's surprise, she learned that Martha Knight and her sister, Belle Schultz, were working on the sets and costumes committee. They had little to do with decision making, though, that was the responsibility of Babbette Fay, a retired costumer.

"You should really get involved," Louise said again and again. "It's so much fun. And you have time on your hands."

Wally had plenty of uses for her time and she just smiled and let Louise's comments go. Sooner or later Nate's time would free up. As the summer progressed, the meetings were likely to stop. It was the nature of committees and summertime. Wally looked forward to it.

She looked at her watch. "I can stay for an hour. Then I have to go home and throw together a salad for dinner. Nate has to go out early tonight."

Louise narrowed her eyes. "You? Throw together a mere salad? Tell me you aren't just talking about serving lettuce and tomatoes and calling it dinner."

"Well, no. It's mixed greens, grilled chicken, walnuts, pears, and some dried cranberries. It'll be filling." She looked at Louise. "Oh, are you mocking me?"

"I wouldn't," said Louise, giving her friend a hug. "It's just that you make us mere meat-and-potatoes people look so boring. But then again, you and your well stocked refrigerator always make me feel inadequate."

Wally shrugged. The reasons for that well stocked refrigerator were still painful, all these years later. Her father had died very young and her mother had gone to work. Wally's grandmother had taken over the childcare for Wally and her brother, but when she died, Wally's mother was unable to deal with the daily responsibilities at home. There was often too little food for dinner and Wally had sworn that when she had a home of her own she would always be ready to feed someone who was hungry. Her reputation had grown among her friends when, at a

23

moment's notice, she could provide an almost complete meal just from her freezer.

She looked at the next customer coming in. "Let me get this one, and you can practice your voice modulation on the person on the phone."

Louise grabbed the receiver and gave a dramatic rendition of "Grove Pharmacy. How may I help you?"

#

Several of the four-year-olds in Wally's day camp class greeted her when she arrived at the town pool. Their mothers and nannies were all sitting together next to the wading pool, talking non-stop, with an assortment of babies and toddlers on their laps or beside them. "Come play with us," one of the little girls said from the edge of the pool. She had also been in Wally's four-year-old class for the school year.

Wally was always sorry to see some of the children go off to kindergarten, and Lila was one of them. But she didn't plan to spend her afternoon with the children, she was here to swim laps and see her own friends. She didn't want to have to say that, though, and she looked over at the adults, hoping one of them would give her a reprieve.

"Lila, come over here and play with Molly. You never get to see her."

Wally gave her a grateful smile, waved at Lila, and went over to the adult pool. She quickly changed direction to walk around the other side, though, when she noticed a heated argument among several residents in her mother-in-law, Tillie's, apartment building. Hoping to get into the water before the group sitting under a large maple tree noticed her, Wally walked quickly to the deep end, shed her cover-up and towel onto a chair, slipped off her rubber flip-flops, and dived into the water.

She surfaced and swam over to the lap lanes. Ducking under the first and second lemon lines, she started doing laps in the empty third lane. But after only two laps, she found herself, when she touched the side of the pool, staring up at the legs of three of Tillie's friends.

"We need you to settle an argument," Orli said.

Wally wanted no part of that. "Is Tillie here?" She was widely regarded as the great mediator in the senior citizen building.

"No."

Wally would have to listen to the problem. She could only hope it would be either so trivial or so obscure that she wouldn't have to say anything.

"Let me get my towel," she said. Walking a bit slower than usual, to give herself a little more time before she got embroiled in what was surely none of her business, she went over to her pool chair. All too soon, she found herself under the tree, listening to Biddy, Orli, and two other women argue.

"Here she is," said Biddy, brushing a bee away from the flower on the housecoat she wore. "Give her a seat."

Feeling ridiculous letting an eighty-year-plus woman get up to give Wally a seat, she went to find one for herself. This wasn't looking good, she thought, if it required sitting to hear.

"Okay," said Wally. She didn't add that she was ready to listen to their problem, because she was surely not and never would be.

Orli seemed to be the spokeswoman. "We need you to settle an argument. Two of us think we should sue and the other two think it's our fault and maybe they should sue us."

"Whom do you want to sue?" Wally asked.

"Neon."

"The restaurant? I thought that was going out of business."

One of the two women who Wally didn't know slapped her own knee and said, "Aha. I told you so."

"If they were going out of business why did they take

our reservation?" Orli asked. She turned to Wally. "We were supposed to have our Welcome Summer dinner there. When we got there, they were closed. And they had our deposit."

"They gave it back," Biddy said, softly.

'That's beside the point," said Orli. "Right, Evelyn?"

Evelyn, who was the knee slapper, nodded. "It is. The point is you wasted our time, you ruined our dinner, and you won't take responsibility for it."

"How could I know they were closing?" said Orli. "When I went to make the arrangements they were busy renovating the restaurant. Who renovates and then closes?"

"Wally knew it was closing," said Evelyn.

"I'd heard a rumor," Wally admitted. The closing of the restaurant, after the brand new chef quit to go work for Wade Fuller's restaurant, Marcella's, was the reason Telly's was about to get a liquor license. "But I hadn't seen a sign or anything. And if they took Orli's deposit..." She didn't bother to finish the sentence. It wouldn't do to make an absolute statement.

Orli, Biddy, and Evelyn started arguing. Wally didn't know what to do. Suddenly Edith, a woman wearing a white flowered rubber bathing cap, who had been dozing nearby, opened her eyes, turned to them, and said, "Let it go. Evelyn, you make the arrangements the next time."

No one argued. Wally said goodbye, and scooted out of there. She was about to dive into the water again when she heard sirens. People got up to see what was going on when the sirens stopped nearby. Wally saw that Tillie's neighbors had gathered their things and were exiting the pool gate just as her phone rang. "Where are you?" asked Louise. She sounded stressed.

"At the pool. What's going on?"

"There was an accident. Martha Knight was hit by a car in the parking lot of Ristorante Marcella."

"That's around the corner," Wally said, grabbing her

things. She wasn't one to chase ambulances, but she felt she had to make sure Martha would be all right. "I'm on my way."

She arrived just in time to see Martha, who was bleeding from her forehead and seemed to have something wrong with her right leg, being worked on by the Grosvenor rescue squad. Wally recognized several of the EMTs. Martha was in good hands.

Orli and company stood nearby, somewhat out of breath. Edith still wore her bathing cap. "Do you know what happened?" Wally asked.

Biddy pointed to a woman who was crying. "She was a witness and she told the police that Martha and her sister were crossing the lot. A white van came from the back of the lot, going really fast, and went straight through to Grove, turning on the next street. It never stopped, just kept going and it was gone before anyone had time to think. Luckily, Wade Fuller was also going to his car. He immediately called 9-1-1 and then tried to help Martha. Maggie Mattoon was across the street, and she called me on my cell phone."

Wondering why Maggie Mattoon had Biddy's number in her phone, Wally looked over and saw Belle, who was surrounded by several people, crying. Wally then saw Belle's daughter, Fergie Schultz, who owned Blossoms, the florist shop across the street, come running out of her store with a roll of paper towels under her arm and an emergency kit. She bent to tend a scratch on her mother's face.

"You don't need to do that," said one of the EMTs. "We'll take care of her next."

"It's okay," said Belle, pushing her daughter's hand away. "I'm all right."

Fergie wrapped her arms around her mother. "I'll drive you to the hospital, Mom," she said. "Just let me go back and lock up."

"Wait," Martha said, holding up her hand from inside

27

the ambulance, "Fergie, take my car key. I don't think I'm going to be able to use it for a while."

Once the ambulance took off for the hospital the crowd began to disperse. That included Orli and company, who headed home for the early-shift dinner. A few remaining bystanders were being questioned by the police. Wally noticed that Dominique Scott, one of the Grosvenor police detectives, and a close personal friend, was talking to some teenagers. She decided to stay to see what developed.

    #

Dominique had worked her way through the group of people standing in the parking lot where Martha Knight's accident occurred, questioning witnesses, when she came toward Wally. For a moment she looked over at her partner, Ryan Devlin, who was working with several officers gathering evidence. He gave her a grim smile in return.

Wally asked Dominique how Martha was doing. "I wasn't able to get a sense of how severe her injuries were before the rescue squad took her to the hospital."

"She hit her head when she fell and I think her leg may be broken," Dominique said, her dark brown eyes showing signs of worry. "But I think she's going to be okay." She paused and looked at Wally. "Getting the guy who hit her is going to be a little more difficult. We have conflicting eye-witness accounts. The only thing that's certain is that the van was plain white, with no writing on it at all." She sighed. "I don't suppose, by any chance, you saw the whole thing and can lead us to the suspect?"

"Sorry. I got here afterward. Louise called to tell me to get over here."

"How did she know?"

"She got a call," Wally said. She looked over at the traffic jam being caused by police redirecting traffic to the side streets. They were keeping Grove Avenue, where the restaurant and parking lot were, clear of cars. Too bad it was nearing rush hour. The way the cars came along the curve down the hill into town, the drivers wouldn't have any idea they were headed into a traffic jam until it was too late to take an alternate route.

Dominique shook her head. "With all these cell phones, you would think someone would have been able to snap a picture of the car as he fled."

Wally shrugged. That bit of technology was still out of her league. Her cell phone was somewhat more basic. "Do you have a clear picture of how it happened?"

"I think so. Martha and her sister were walking from the florist shop across the street to Martha's car." Dominique turned to look at Blossoms. "Her niece owns the shop. Apparently they stopped for some time to talk to a friend before crossing the street."

"That's right," said Wally. She looked at the row of cars parked in the lot. They were on the side of a through lane that ran from Grove to First, the parallel street behind the restaurant. First Street was used for most rear of the store deliveries, leaving room for shoppers to park in front. "So the driver was parked in the lot and didn't see the women when he was pulling out? Or did he cut through from First?"

"We're not sure."

"It's lucky Martha wasn't hit head on, or worse, both of them."

"It could have been all three of them," Dominique said. "Wade Fuller was in the lot too, not far behind the two women. He jumped out of the way when he heard the car and shouted for the ladies to watch out."

Wally looked over at the newly refurbished restaurant known as Ristorante Marcella. Wade had spared no expense in the remodeling; leaded glass windows and doors in glossy mahogany frames made the restaurant seem more open than it had been before. Cream-colored stucco with strategically placed "age spots" gave a Tuscan feel, and

29

cheerful flowers in ancient looking pottery added to the northern Italian feel. As much as the restaurant looked brand new, it still looked as if it had been there for centuries.

The parking lot they were standing on was also brand new, as the scent of the blacktop baking in the sun attested. It was a new configuration, Wally knew, since the former parking lot, which had been primarily behind the building, had been transformed into an outdoor garden for dining al fresco. A line of tall cypress trees and a fence completely screened it from the street, ensuring privacy.

Dominique started walking toward her partner. "Let's see what Ryan knows."

Ryan didn't look happy when he saw Wally and Dominique headed in his direction. Wally didn't have to guess why—she had solved a few of his cases. Add to that his touch of resentment toward her son-in-law Elliot, who had been Dominique's partner before becoming an assistant district attorney, and it was understandable why Ryan grumbled something about civilians getting involved.

Wally felt uncomfortable stepping on Ryan's toes. And it was unnecessary. She didn't know anything about who could have committed the hit-and-run.

"Ryan," Dominique said, in a tone that indicated she understood his feelings, "could you please show me where each of the three people was standing at the time of the accident?"

He led the way up the central lane of the parking lot. There was a drop of blood on the asphalt but, Wally noticed, no skid marks, and no pieces of the vehicle. Three chalk marked Xs indicated where Martha, Belle, and Wade Fuller had been when the car went by.

"Were the two women together?" Wally asked, noting the two Xs about ten feet ahead of the single X.

"Yes."

"Wade was behind them, right? The driver could

probably see him, but not Belle and Martha?"

Ryan nodded. "I suppose. There is an incline over here. They would have been out of the driver's line of sight, lower than Mr. Fuller, even more so than their smaller stature would indicate."

"So Wade jumped out of the way and the driver ran right into Martha?" Wally frowned.

"That's where you're wrong," said Ryan.

Wally and Dominique stared at each other, then at Ryan.

"She wasn't hit by the van," Ryan said. "Mr. Fuller says it missed them. Mrs. Knight admitted she tripped when she was pulling Mrs. Schultz out of the way, and Mrs. Schultz fell on top of her, pushing Mrs. Knight's head onto the driveway. And Mr. Fuller feels terrible about it. He said he reacted in self-preservation, but if he had known the van would nearly hit those women, he'd have stood his ground."

Wally had a horrible mental image of Wayne being hit head on by a van. It would have been terrible and possibly fatal. The reality that no one was struck was a huge relief. "Then this isn't a hit-and-run?" Wally asked. "Does that mean you aren't going to investigate?"

"We'll still look into it, but there is no evidence to gather," Ryan said. He seemed disappointed. "At worst, it was reckless driving, maybe because the parking lot was recently reconfigured."

"I hope you catch whoever did this anyway," said Wally, as she turned to go. She was about to open her mouth again when she thought better of it and decided to stick to her MYOB resolution. All she said was, "I wish you good luck."

Chapter Four

"You simply can't refuse, Wally," Louise said. She had called twice earlier in the day while Wally was out, and now that Wally had called her back, Louise wasn't taking no for an answer. "Martha can't finish working on the sets and she was Babbette's whole staff. You'll have to pitch in."

"But I don't know anything about set design."

"Neither does Martha, believe me. All she was doing was filling in the colors on the design that Babbette sketched out. You can do that. And you can help reupholster the wing back chair and the sofa. I think all they're going to do is staple new fabric over the old. The whole thing is practically finished already."

It sounded easy enough, both the painting and the reupholstering, but then again, all of Louise's schemes sounded easy until they were actually underway. On the other hand, if Martha could handle set painting, maybe Wally could too.

She almost shook herself. What was she thinking? Was she agreeing to this? Surely someone else could take over Martha's responsibilities, right?

"Wally?" Louise asked. "Are you still there?"

"I'm thinking."

"Could you do it louder?"

Nate came into the kitchen. He took one look at Wally's scowl and said, "What's going on?"

She covered the phone. "Louise wants me to help

32

paint the sets for the play. Martha is out of commission."

"Sounds like fun," Nate said. Wally took a closer look at him to see if he'd lost his mind, but he looked about the same to her. Stressed, actually, but he'd been that way for several weeks now. Still, maybe he had a point. It could be fun. Maybe.

She uncovered the phone, took an I-must-be-crazy breath, and spoke to Louise. "How about if I go with you to see if I can do the work? Then I'll decide."

"Are you doubting me?"

"No, of course not. It's just that there may be other factors to consider. For all you know, someone else is anxious to take over for Martha. I wouldn't want to step on any toes."

"Sure, sure," Louise said. "I'll be right over."

Wally and Louise were in Louise's convertible on their way over to the church-turned-theater when they saw Fred Neimeyer walking up the street. Louise pulled over to say hi and gave Fred a promotional speech for the show. "It's going to be great," she said. "Funny too. Who doesn't like a good laugh?"

"I wouldn't think those amateur shows are very good," Fred said. "It's not for me."

Louise gave Wally a knowing look. Fred hadn't gotten the nickname, Naysayer, for nothing.

"Uh, Wally," he said, "is Nate at home?"

"He's either there or in the barn," Wally told him. "Do you need something?"

"Um, not really. I just wanted to say hi."

"Have fun then," Wally said. It was about all she could get in since Louise had already waved goodbye to Fred and pulled back onto the street. Wally had no time to wonder what Fred wanted from Nate as Louise sped over to the theater.

For the next two weeks Wally worked every day after

nursery camp to help Babbette Fay get the sets ready for the productions. Babbette had a background in the theater and told many interesting stories about theater life in the seventies and eighties. She was surprisingly superstitious. Wally was amazed at the concessions Babbette made to theater ghosts. "I'm not the only one," Babbette told Wally.

"That's why Lance always gets a bunch of us to watch the last scene of the play," Babbette explained. "The last line of the play must never be rehearsed without an audience. If he can't get a make-believe audience, he won't permit the last line of the play to be read."

Wally was amazed by how much she learned about paint and fabric and stage directions and by how seriously the cast and crew took their jobs even though it was an amateur production. Working behind the scenes on the set crew turned out to be more interesting than she'd thought. She enjoyed observing the dynamics of the troupe. The director impressed her as he tried to evoke certain emotions from people, soothe other's sore feelings, and coax others to forgive the insults heaped upon them by Courtney, who obviously considered herself the real director. But it was clear to everyone else who was in charge. Lance was on top of everything, from the smallest button or prop to the incessantly running toilets in the balcony-level bathrooms.

The play began to gel, which, Wally had to admit, was exciting. Though Louise had no real part in it, since Courtney Haven was the lead and Louise only the understudy, Louise was ever present, hanging on every word Lance Palmer uttered. The play was scheduled to open in four weeks, the second and third weekends in September, on both Friday and Saturday nights. Anyone with end-of-summer vacation plans was advised to cancel them.

That was when Wally drew the line. Because of her teaching and day camp schedules, the only time she and

Nate had to go away for several weeks at a time was at the end of the summer. She looked forward to that time all year, when she could spend whole days and nights with her husband and have no distractions to pull them away from each other.

Lance Palmer understood. "Look, I really appreciate how you pitched in. You've made a big difference. Finish whatever you can, and we'll muddle through with the rest."

At that point Wally would have canceled her plans for Lance. Luckily, that was unnecessary, since there was little left to do.

    #

"How is your Aunt Martha feeling?" Wally asked Fergie, when she walked into Blossoms. She was there to order flowers for Tillie's birthday and figured she could ask Martha's niece, who owned the shop, for an update.

Fergie frowned. "She'll be okay, but her leg was really shattered. She had surgery to reassemble it. They had to put in rods."

Wally had heard that. "Will she be going to a rehab facility soon?"

"Yes, next week."

"That's a good sign, isn't it?"

"I suppose. But it was such a nightmare. Who could have imagined they'd be crossing the parking lot at the same exact time as someone came shooting through it? They had left my store long before that. I should have walked them to the car myself." She shuddered. "Did you know I'm named for Martha? Fergie is for my middle name." She sighed. "It's got my mother all upset. And she insists on visiting Aunt Martha every day."

Wally could understand that. Belle was a quiet, needy type, while her sister was a ball of fire. If not for Martha, Belle would sit home all the time. She depended on other people to get around, since she never got a driver's license and didn't particularly like to take mass transit by herself.

35

That meant Fergie had to make time in her daily schedule to drive her mother to the hospital to see Martha.

"I could drive her over one day if you can't manage," Wally said. "It must be hard running a business by yourself."

Fergie blinked at Wally. "To tell you the truth, right now business isn't so hot. I've had two parties cancel on me." She narrowed her eyes and glared out the store front window. Wally had the distinct impression it was in the direction of Ristorante Marcella.

"The accident caused you to lose business?" Wally asked, wondering how that could be.

She received a puzzled look in response to her inane question. Then the light seemed to dawn on Fergie and she shook her head. "No, not that. He discouraged two people who were having gatherings at his restaurant from buying from me. After I had spent time doing a proposal. And he's disparaged me to several party planners. Without the weekly orders from the synagogues and small orders like yours, I'd be sitting around twiddling my thumbs."

"Are you talking about Wade Fuller? Why would he do that?"

The guilty look on Fergie's face was Wally's answer. She didn't want to know the details. Rumors about Wade and his adulterous behavior weren't news, and Wally was sorry Fergie had gotten involved.

"Why does he do anything?" she said. "Because he has the power."

The door to the street opened and another customer came in. Wally quickly placed her order and got out of Fergie's way.

Nate was in the kitchen when Wally came home. He'd been so busy lately she was surprised to see him, and she didn't waste a moment before giving him a hug.

"Have you finally finished all that work?" she asked.

"Not even close. And I have an emergency board

meeting tonight about the performing arts center." He dipped his head. "I'm sorry I'm so busy. I miss you."

"I miss you too. So I'm going to let you take me out to dinner. We'll go to Telly's and afterward you can go to your meeting. At least we'll have a few minutes together."

"You're on."

It was early for Wally and Nate to be eating, but since Nate had the meeting to go to they arrived at Telly's at a quarter to seven. It was already fairly crowded with families with young children but Wally and Nate were given a table right away. While they looked over the menu, Wally looked for Telly. She wanted his take on the evening's specials.

The server, Stacey, a single mom in her mid-thirties, came to tell them the specials. She gave them time to make their choices and came back a few minutes later, all without Wally seeing Telly. Wally asked for him and Stacy gave her a warning look. "He isn't in a good mood," Stacey said. "He got some bad news."

Nate had been looking at his menu but his head came up when he heard that. "Is he in his office?" Without waiting, he stood up. "I'm sorry, Wally, but I promise I'll be right back."

"Give Telly my regards," Wally called after him. To Stacey she said, "I think we'll need a few more minutes."

Wally gazed out the window and watched as people arrived for dinner. But then she noticed Rolly Sherman, in ragged sweats, standing in the middle of the road, with a beer can in his hand, directing the evening traffic. Stacey had seen it too, Wally realized, because she pulled out her cell phone, punched in a number and went outside. After signaling traffic to stop, she helped Rolly to the curb. A few moments later the police arrived to take him into custody.

When Stacey came back into the restaurant, Wally,

whose heart was still racing from the danger of it all, motioned her over.

"Can I get you something?" she asked.

"No, I just wanted to say thanks for taking care of Rolly. He could have been hit by a car."

"He's done that nearly every day for the past few weeks," she said, showing a bit of the exasperation she must feel, "unless he's in jail. He's almost as bad as after the car accident. And doing it here, in front of the restaurant, where the cars are coming down the hill and around the curve is even more dangerous. If the drivers try to make the light they might be going too fast to avoid him."

Wally agreed, and was sorry to hear that this had happened before. "I thought he was rehabilitated."

Stacey nodded. "He was. He even had a job and we sometimes went to the movies together. But lately…" She frowned. "Look, he's harmless and we can't just let him stand there. Whoever sees him first usually takes care of it." She went off to take care of another customer.

Nate had returned. He didn't look happy.

"What happened?" she asked, after they had finally given their order.

"Wade Fuller. He got the liquor license that had been promised to Telly."

"How did that happen?"

Nate's frown deepened. "He paid a quarter of a million dollars for it, the most anyone has ever paid for a liquor license in this town."

"Did Telly think he was going to get it for free? Maybe he should have made an offer."

"He did make a good one. He showed me the papers when we talked about increasing his insurance to account for the license. I thought it would be no problem. But apparently it was not nearly enough."

"You mean it's open for bids? I thought you had to be

on a list and when your name came up you had right of first refusal."

"Not really, although ordinarily it works out fairly. Not this time. Wade Fuller got the license. The official notice came today. At this very moment he is probably popping open a cork to celebrate." Nate sounded bitter, as bitter as Telly most likely sounded telling him the story.

"Where does Wade get all his money?" Wally asked. "First he renovates his whole restaurant, hires away a four star chef from Neon, then he pays a lot of money to buy the liquor license. Meanwhile he's running around on his wife and giving grief to struggling shop keepers."

Nate put down the roll he had been eating and gave her one of his blue-green-eyed stares. "What are you talking about?"

Wally filled him in on her conversation with Fergie. "He's been a busy guy," she concluded. "And on top of all that, which would be enough to keep two people busy, he's chairing the performing arts center committee."

"Don't remind me."

"Is that what's been bothering you? Is he causing trouble?"

"I don't think he knows how to do anything other than cause trouble, for a lot of people. He even lured away some of Telly's best workers."

"Please tell me Alberto isn't one of them," Wally said. He was the only busperson who would blow up balloons for the children and twist them into cute shapes.

"Sorry, he's at Wade's now." Nate shook his head. "But don't worry about me. I'm a big boy and I can take care of myself."

#

The rehearsals were moving right along. Although some people had misgivings, it had worked out well to cast Paul and Casey Clark in the roles of the young lovers. They were about thirty, the age of the characters in the play, believable actors, and new to the town of Grosvenor. This would give them a good chance to meet people, Wally thought. She still remembered when she and Nate had moved into town from Brooklyn. They knew no one, but when they joined the Newcomers Club that all changed. Many of the people they had met back then were still among their friends.

Several other young people filled the parts of the three friends of each of the leads and of the secretary and maid, and they were all becoming acquainted. Doug Norton, the man who had been chosen to play the father of the boyfriend, was also competent in his role, and a constant source of jokes. Wally only wished she could remember them long enough to tell them to Nate when she got home.

On Tuesday, August fifteenth, when Wally finished the last detail and labeled everything for the stage crew, she felt a sudden change in atmosphere come over the company. Seeking an explanation, she went to find Louise.

Her friend sat smiling in the chair designated for Courtney. "What are you doing?" Wally asked. "If she catches you in that chair we are all going to have to listen to her tirades."

"No problem," said Louise. "She isn't here and she isn't coming any time soon. She called Lance and told him she had everything under control, didn't have to rehearse endlessly with the amateurs, and needed to rest. She'll be back after Labor Day.

Louise would get her chance to be the star, at least for rehearsals. And Lance was swearing to everyone that he wouldn't take Courtney back, no matter what. He even sent Louise roses, with a card that read, "To my new leading lady."

"I know Lance will let her play the role when she gets back," Louise said at rehearsal the next day. "But this is more fun than I can imagine."

"I'm glad you're happy. We'll record it before I go

40

away, so you'll have it to remember."

#

A phone ringing at seven a.m. is never good news, Wally thought as she dashed dripping wet out of the bathroom and picked it up.

"It's ruined," Louise wailed.

Trying to hang onto her bath towel and still talk, Wally asked, "What is?"

"The play. The theater. The upstairs bathroom flooded and it's all ruined." Louise sounded close to tears. "I knew it was too good to be true."

Wally remembered all the times Lance had complained about the noise of the balcony level toilets running on and on. "How do you know there was a flood?"

"Maggie Mattoon called me. She couldn't wait to spread the word. A jogger going by at five saw water pooling outside the doors and called the police. They went in and found that one of the toilets had overflowed and everything was soaked. She said it wasn't pretty."

"Maggie told you all this? How did she find out?"

"Have you forgotten that her husband is on the township committee."

Wally did know that, but not necessarily at seven in the morning, before her coffee. "Maybe it isn't so bad. Maybe once they clean it up it'll be okay. There are still three and a half weeks left."

"Don't be such a Pollyanna," Louise snapped. "I know it's over. That's it." She hung up. Wally did not call back. What could she possibly say? They'd have to sort it all out later.

When Nate came in from his walk with Sammy, she told him about the flood. To her surprise, he looked truly disappointed. "I really wanted to see Louise in action," he said. He reached for Wally to give her a hug. "And of course all the wonderful work you did." He pulled away, looking pensive. "I think I'll go over see what's going on."

41

Wally headed for the stairs. "Wait five minutes and I'll go with you. We can get breakfast in town afterward and I can still get to work on time." There were only two days of day camp left, and Wally didn't want to miss them. It was the last time she'd see most of the children.

There was a small crowd outside the former church watching a crew set up a suction pump when Wally and Nate arrived. Babbette Fay was there and Wally went to speak to her. She had tears in her eyes.

"Our beautiful work is gone," she sobbed. "I knew we hadn't done enough to appease them."

"Who?"

Babbette leaned close to Wally. "The ghosts. They're always here and we did not appease them. See what happened?"

"Maybe it isn't so bad," Wally said, hoping she was right, for everyone's sake.

Large fans to help evaporate the remaining moisture stood waiting to be brought inside. Every door and window had been opened. Nate spoke to a few people and reported back that luckily, it wasn't a backed up sewer pipe as Maggie had claimed, but a burst water pipe. It had indeed flooded the theater causing severe damage—the stage was warped beyond repair. Several flats in the storeroom had been soaked as water ran down them, and some of the furniture had been torn when the pieces were removed from the path of the flood.

"You're saying that the sets, props, and almost everything else is fine, but that the theater is unusable?"

Nate nodded. "Yes. But I'm sure you can find another place to hold the play. There are lots of auditoriums in town."

"What do you mean 'You can find another place?'"

"Okay, maybe not you. But someone can. Call Louise. I'll bet she'll line up another place in less than an hour."

Wally didn't think it would be that easy, but she called Louise anyway. The whoops of joy that resulted nearly deafened her. Louise promised to get right on it. "I'll call Lance and tell him the good news," she said.

Louise wasn't singing the same happy tune when Wally got home from work. "We can't have it in any of the schools," she said, "because they will be in session by then. Plus our sets will only fit in the high school which already has a concert scheduled."

"What about another church?" Wally asked. She knew the synagogues were out because they couldn't be used on Friday nights, since it would be Shabbat, and not until too late for a Saturday night performance, for the same reason. Sunset would still be relatively late when the play was scheduled.

"No dice. And the community center is still undergoing renovation."

"Did you try the movie theater?" Wally suggested. "It used to be a playhouse."

"Has it slipped your mind that they chopped it into tiny little theaters no bigger than your living room?"

She had a point. Wally couldn't think of anything else right at the moment, as much as she wanted to help, so she said she'd keep her thinking cap on.

"Tell Nate to put his on too," Louise begged. "I'm also telling Norman. One of us should be able to think of something."

Wally hoped that was true.

43

Chapter Five

"You should cancel your trip," Louise said. She had brought fresh bagels and muffins early Sunday morning to Wally and Nate's. She had supplemented the breads with a spread of fish and cream cheese, enough for six people at least, and a pleading look on her face.

Nate peeked into the bag, looking, no doubt, for his favorite kind of bagel. But Wally didn't want to accept Louise's offering, especially if it came with a price tag. "Beware friends with agendas bearing gifts," she muttered to Nate.

"I don't think so," Wally said to Louise, while trying to wrestle the bagels away from her ever-hungry husband. "We deserve this time off, and I can't wait—school will start all too soon."

"But we need you to help get the sets and props ready for the show. If you don't help we may as well not have asked for permission to use the new theater."

Wally still couldn't believe that Norman and Nate had convinced the theater board to allow *Anyone Else* to be produced before the scheduled opening of the performing arts center. She'd heard at length the fight that Wade Fuller had waged against the idea, and was pleased that the other board members took Nate and Norman's side. She only wished she could have been there.

Reality set in. Wally was going to have to do it.

"You don't mind giving up your vacation?" she asked Nate.

44

"I really don't think we have a choice. Not because of the play, although it's a factor. I've been thinking that I'd better stay around and make sure Wade doesn't pull any other stunts before the theater opens." He had tried a few, much to Nate's and Norman's vexation.

Louise smiled. "Great. Okay, you two, enjoy your breakfast. Wally, I'll see you bright and early tomorrow at the theater." With that she left, leaving Nate smiling over his surprise breakfast and Wally shaking her head.

#

When Wally walked into the new Grosvenor Performing Arts Center the next morning she was immediately impressed. Though it wasn't quite finished, she could see the clean lines and attention to detail which extended from the front door all the way into the theater and up to the stage. Workmen scurried about laying carpet and installing seats. Several people wearing t-shirts imprinted with STAFF sat on chairs listening to instructions.

Kaylin Irish, the operations manager, finished talking about ticket sales and reservations and turned the meeting over to Harvey Floyd, the production manager, who reminded Wally of a young George Clooney. He told them that the newly slotted production was making completion of the performing arts center go at an undesirably frenetic pace, but that the production of the play would be a good soft-opening test for the space before the magic show that was to be the premiere event. They could only stage the play once, but the theater staff was willing to help in any way they could. Wally felt a little thrill to be part of all this history.

She went backstage and looked for Babbette. There was no one there in what was obviously some type of workroom. Wally knew that Babbette needed to make extensive repairs to the sets and props, all outside, per none other than Wade Fuller, but she couldn't figure out where

Babbette could be.

Louise appeared next to Wally. "I have to go back on from the other side," she explained. Wally remembered the scene. This was an easier transition than it had been in the old theater.

"Before you go," Wally said, "have you seen Babbette?"

"Out back."

There was no chance to ask her anything else, because Louise was already going back on stage, saying Courtney's next line.

Wally followed the exit signs for the back of the theater. She ended up in an open space behind the theater that was in between it and a line of stores on Grove Street. She had never been back there and it was a surprise to find the old-fashioned, wooden rear staircases that led up from the ground to the apartments over the stores.

"I'm glad you found me," Babbette said. "I should have left you a map."

A breeze riffled the newspapers beneath the furniture Babbette was painting. "I can't believe Wade wouldn't let me work with paint inside the theater. He's so afraid I'll mess it up." She reached for another paper before it could blow away. "At least he can't make me wallpaper the panels outside. They are way too heavy to move that far." She held up a paintbrush and pointed to the ragged looking chair that needed to be transformed. The thin fabric on it had disintegrated after it was hauled out of the flooded church. "Here you go." She looked up at the sky, where the sun was beating down. "Once this is finished we can go inside to work on that wallpapering. Harvey is being really nice and offered to help."

Wally could barely wait to see how that was going to work as she followed Babbette to the door and held it for her, since she had a prop in her hands.

Babbette stopped at the doorway and rested the prop

46

while she took a flower from a small vase and placed it just to the left of the door jamb. Then she went inside.

"May I ask why you did that?" said Wally.

"I'm not taking any chances. I'm going to placate whatever theater ghosts are here."

"But it's a brand-new theater. There couldn't be any ghosts."

A raised eyebrow was followed by, "How can you be so sure?"

Wally dropped the subject.

At three o'clock Tillie, Orli, and Biddy came into the theater, wide-eyed and chattering about how beautiful it was. Harvey offered to give them a tour. After checking him out head to toe, they happily agreed. They were back forty minutes later. "It's beautiful, Wally. So impressive," said Tillie. "You should have gone with us."

"Tsk," said Orli. "I forgot to ask about the concession. Now where did Harvey go?"

"Let's go find him," Tillie said.

They came back five minutes later looking totally perplexed, upset and confused. "He can't do it, can he, Wally?" Tillie said.

It was a toss-up on which question to ask first. Wally went with both. "He, who? What?"

Biddy spoke first. "Wade Fuller."

"I should have known," Wally said. "What has he done now?"

"He said we cannot have any food or drinks in the theater. I saw them building the concession stand for the movie theaters, so obviously there will be food in the building. Why can't we have any?"

Orli shook her head. "No refreshments? What's next with this guy?"

Wally sighed. "He's worried about damage."

"Muffins and coffee are not likely to cause damage," Orli said. "Unless you think they put down a carpet that is liable to stain."

"How stupid can they be?" asked Biddy. "Don't they have any sense? All this money and they can't figure out you don't put down a carpet like that?"

Orli reached out her hand to stop her friend's blather. "I didn't say they did, dear. I said I thought they probably hadn't."

Wally turned to Tillie. "Did you explain to Wade what you will be selling?"

"Yes. He said he didn't care if we held our bake sale outside, or in the middle of Grove Avenue, but that there was no way we could do it in the lobby."

"But what if it rains?" asked Orli.

"I asked him that. He said get an umbrella."

"I'm not sitting outside," said Biddy. "It could be ninety-five degrees out there. I want to sit in the air conditioning."

"Maybe you should cancel the sale," said Wally.

"No, we will not. It is a fundraiser for the youth theater. It is done every year when the show goes on and we aren't going to be the first people to let them down."

"Do you want me to go talk to him?" Wally asked, not sure she wanted to at all, and not sure there would be any point to trying.

Their answer was immediate and unanimous. "Yes."

\#

Wally had no intention of subjecting herself to Wade Fuller's snide personality, and she felt she had a strong case for asking Nate to intervene on behalf of his mother's charity.

Before she had a chance to call him, though, or even decide if she really wanted him to get involved, she saw surprise on the faces of the three women facing her. Her back was to the door and she turned to see what the ladies were looking at. Her stomach dropped. There, coming in to the theater, trailing perfume vapors and sashaying for all she was worth, was Courtney Haven. Or, Wally mused, should she think of her as the new improved Courtney Haven? The woman's skin was stretched tighter than an artist's canvas. In the sunlight from the glass-fronted building, Wally could see faint remnants of the bruising Courtney's face must have experienced after she had her skin tailored to fit.

"Oh, no," said Tillie.

"This can't be good," said Biddy.

"Louise is going to be so upset," said Orli.

They were all right, of course. Wally had only one other thought. But, she realized, since fleeing was out of the question, she'd better see what she could do to help. She was halfway to the stage when the moment happened. There was nothing she could do but stop short and watch the drama unfold.

Unfortunately, Tillie and friends also had their eyes riveted on the action in front of them and they didn't notice that Wally had stopped. There was a collision, followed by accusations and apologies, and Wally missed the confrontation between Courtney and Louise. But, by the look on Louise's face as she fled into the wings, it was most unpleasant, at least for one of them.

"Let's go girls," Orli cried. She pushed past Wally and headed for the backstage area. Wally found herself trailing behind the three women, who walked two abreast, leaving no room for Wally to get around them. She was pretty sure Louise didn't want to have to face them all, so she skittered through one of the rows of seats and came out in front of the ladies, begging them to let her see Louise alone.

She had just reached the dressing room, a luxury no one had ever expected when the play was first being rehearsed, when she saw Lance arguing with Courtney. "You can't just waltz in here weeks later and expect to pick up where you left off. You've been replaced, darling, and I have a new star."

"You have a simple housewife, not an actress."

Wally was pretty sure that housewife was the last descriptor on Louise's personal list and she suspected Louise would have a few things to say on the subject.

"And what are you?" asked Lance before Louise could reply. "Didn't you say you were 'taking time off from acting to raise a family,' oh, about seventeen years ago? Do you even have a SAG card?"

Courtney turned on her heel and went back onto the stage. "Excuse me," she called out. "Who here would prefer to have that frumpy redhead play the lead, over me?"

"This is not casting by democratic vote," Lance growled from behind her. The look on his face was murderous, but he did not shout. "Come backstage and maybe we can sort this out."

Courtney smiled, reminding Wally of Nate when he had a no-lose hand in a game of Hearts. "I thought you'd see it my way," Courtney said.

Wally didn't stick around to listen to the negotiations. She had a friend to console.

Chapter Six

Wally was surprised to see Louise at her front door when she got home from setting up her classroom for the fall term at the nursery school. Louise had moped for days, but today she looked positively cheery. Wally invited her in to have lunch with her, hoping to learn what had changed.

"Okay," said Louise, "but just something quick. We have to get over to rehearsals."

"Rehearsals are in the evening," Wally pointed out. "People work during the day."

"Right, but not all day. There are two people who can't come to rehearsals during the day. You and I are going to stand in for them."

"I'm no actress," said Wally. "I couldn't."

"Don't worry. You won't be standing in for an actor. You'll be on stage crew."

"That sounds like fun."

Louise slapped her hand on the table. "I knew you'd get into this."

Wally hadn't really needed Louise to point that out. She had been really looking forward to seeing the play. She realized as she made them each a small salad of cottage cheese and fruit, with a side of mini-muffins baked with the last of the season's blueberries, that she'd missed working on it.

After their salads, Louise limited herself to two of Wally's cookies, her personal bare minimum, since she was in such a hurry to get to the theater. Wally had no choice but to hurry too.

When they arrived they found Lance Palmer in a murderous mood. "Courtney," he shouted, "this scene is about Mrs. Corbett realizing she has been tricked by her daughter. If you can't manage to show some emotion, then I will get someone who can." He turned to scan the onlookers and, spotting Louise, smiled. "We can make the change immediately."

Louise looked ready to run up onto the stage, but went to sit in the audience instead. Wally sat beside her, waiting for instructions.

Courtney cast a deadly glance in Louise's direction. Louise wiggled her fingers in a friendly response, while muttering under her breath.

After doing the scene two more times, with a bit more conviction on Courtney's part, Lance called for a break. Louise and Wally went over to see how they could fill in for the people who weren't present.

"Louise," he said, "my darling, you will play the part of the maid, since Hillary can't be here until later. We will start from the opening scene of the play." He turned to Wally. "You will work with the stage crew. Get your instructions from them."

Louise was not the understudy for the role of the maid, but she knew the script by heart. She went backstage. Wally followed, looking for Babbette, the head of the crew.

"Don't worry about a thing," said Babbette. "I'll tell you what to do after the scene."

Wally watched the opening of the play. Louise came on to say the first line. The stage had a large wingback chair slightly off center stage, and doors on all three walls, some glass, with a verdant background behind. An ice bucket with a wine bottle in it was next to the chair and there were other smaller chairs, little tables, a few lamps, and assorted knickknacks. Several vases stood on the tables. They would have silk flowers in them for the performance, adding even more color and realism to the scene. Wally admired the set, which had turned out beautifully, especially in the new surroundings. And she admired her friend, who was giving it her all, even though she lost the part she wanted most.

Louise entered from stage right holding a duster. She gave a few half-hearted swipes at the tables and plumped the cushions on the couch, all the while looking at the chair. She said her lines, gave another swipe to the chair and turned, giving a little backward kick as she left the stage. It set the tone for the play, which was a farce, and had the group laughing. When it was played for real by the young woman who had the part, she would be wearing a low-cut, tight French maid's uniform.

As Louise was leaving the stage, Courtney entered. Maybe it was the competition, maybe it was professionalism, but this time she played her role well. It might not make Louise happy, Wally thought as she got ready to move the scenery, but it was good for the play. Let the show go on.

#

Before Wally was ready, school was back in session. As she herded her new students into their classroom for the first day, Wally thought of the other children who had so recently left. They were starting kindergarten now, just as Jodi, Wally's granddaughter had, a few days earlier. For some reason, that made Wally more emotional than usual.

She pulled herself together and looked around the room at the little faces in front of her. Many of them had been in the school before, and Wally knew their names, but some were new. It was her job to get them to be a cohesive class, and she got right to it.

Ordinarily in the afternoons of the first weeks of school, Wally stayed afterward in case any parent wanted to talk about problems. This year, because of the play,

Wally authorized the school secretary to give out her cell phone number. She had to be at the rehearsals, since the stage crew person she was subbing for had a full-time job, but she also wanted to be available, if necessary.

Fortunately, everything was going smoothly and they were ready for the show. Tillie had told her the tickets were selling well. Orli and Biddy had solicited baked goods from everyone they could think of, with the exception of Renee Stein. "You shouldn't know from her muffins," Biddy had said. "Lead. Pure lead." They'd asked Nate to set up a table outside the theater, following Wade's ban of their sales inside, and decided that they would only run it before the show and during the intermission, since they didn't want to miss the play.

Lance addressed the group at the end of the rehearsal. He seemed genuinely moved when he thanked everyone for their efforts and predicted a good show. "So many of you have gone above and beyond, and I am grateful. You may not all be the stars of the show, but in my mind you are stars to me." He paused. "Two days. Let's be ready."

#

When Wally got home, expecting to see Nate rooting through the fridge for a snack, the kitchen was empty. She looked in the driveway and saw that his car was gone, but he hadn't left a note.

A feeling that something was out of whack came over her. She couldn't put her finger on it. Most of the time Nate was his usual self, but lately he would get quiet and pensive, and he'd be gone for hours without much explanation. He also got phone calls that he left the room to take. That had rarely happened before. She was going to have to sit him down and get to the bottom of whatever it was.

Wally took the opportunity to go for a walk with Sammy. As always, he pulled her along at a steady clip for the first half of their walk, as if his dinner bowl were on

54

Grove Avenue and he was anxious to get to it. Then he settled down, making the walk a lot more pleasurable. At that hour Wally enjoyed walking through the park, watching the children of various ages playing soccer on the different fields. She saw some former students waving to her and waved back. The warm sun and the smell of the drying leaves, a few of which skittered past her and swirled in the light breeze, were some of the best parts of the late summer. Wally appreciated every moment. She was pretty sure Sammy appreciated it too, in his own doggy way.

Nate was back when she got home and had started cutting up vegetables for a salad. Wally took the leftover poached salmon from the refrigerator and finished the salad with smoked Gouda cheese, dried cranberries, walnuts, and sliced pears. There was no need to heat up the kitchen this evening.

"How was your day?" Wally asked, hoping there would be an opportunity to talk about whatever was bothering Nate.

"Fine, and yours?"

This wasn't going well. If it were anyone else, Wally would wonder if her marriage might have a problem. She tried again. "So what's new?"

"The Singers are moving out of town," Nate said as he filled glasses of iced tea for each of them.

"Where did you hear that?"

Nate looked up from what he was doing, nearly spilling one of the glasses. "Let me think. I guess Fred Neimeyer mentioned it."

"When did you see him?"

"Oh, in town. I ran into him."

"Did he say whether his divorce is final yet?" Fred Neimeyer was in the nastiest divorce battle that Wally had ever heard of, outside of that of a celebrity. Wally had sympathy for both sides, but mostly the children.

Nate placed two napkins on the table. "He didn't say."

Wally detected an odd note in his response. She turned away from the refrigerator, where she was looking for dressing. "Nate, is something going on with Fred?"

"I can't really say."

"Are you helping him?" This was getting frustrating.

"I certainly hope so." Nate carried their salads over to the table. "These look great, let's eat."

Chapter Seven

Before she knew it, the day of the performance had arrived. Wally had taken the day off so she wouldn't miss a minute of the preparations.

Lance sent everyone home after an early morning dress rehearsal and told them to get some rest. "I don't want anyone running errands and getting tired, and no one should have a big lunch. I want you lean and mean for the show."

Doug Norton was the first actor changed back into his street clothes. He waved at Wally as he and Lance, who was staying at Doug's house for the final days of the rehearsals, left to go relax.

Wally and Louise sent themselves over to the nail salon for manicures and pedicures. Courtney had mentioned she was getting her nails done too, but luckily she chose one of the half dozen or so other nail salons in town. Two of the other female cast members also chose the same salon as Wally and Louise, and there was a bit of a wait while they all got their places sorted out. Wally ended up getting her manicure first, while Louise went right into a pedicure chair.

Ticket sales had gone well, but the theater, being larger than the original venue, still had seats available. Or at least it did, until Louise's nails were dry, because she managed to get so many people interested just by talking about the show that the box office was besieged by cell phone calls, all originating in the salon.

"You've got to calm down," Wally advised her friend.

"Or you'll be too tired to enjoy the show." Wally knew there were special appreciations in store for Louise, since she'd had a sneak peek of the program. Lance had insisted on thanking Louise by name, giving her full credit for saving the show.

#

"Let's grab lunch," Louise said when they were done. "And then I promise to rest."

They went into the Grove Diner, and took a booth. Wally ordered her usual tuna melt and tried to feel guilt free about it. Louise, as part of her personal makeover, which had lasted far longer than any of her previous personal makeovers, ordered a Greek salad.

Louise filched a French fry from Wally's plate. "Did you make sure that Nate doesn't have any late clients coming? Will he be there on time?" She dipped the fry into the little pool of ketchup that Wally had poured and took a bite.

Wally turned her plate so Louise had easier access to the fries. "Yes, he'll be there. I trust you told Norman to be on time?"

"I did. Actually, I told him the curtain was going up a 7:30 rather than 8:00. That's the best way to get him there on time." She took another fry. "We have to pick up Tillie and company by five, so we can get them set up."

It was probably a bit early, Wally thought, but she wasn't going to argue. At least the women would have had time to have dinner by then. They had all switched with four o'clockers, as the people on the early dinner shift were called, so they could have their dinners. Skipping them was out of the question. Wally, Nate, Louise, and Norman would be eating much later since they were planning to go out to dinner after the show.

Wally's mother-in-law, Tillie, along with Orli and Biddy, were waiting outside when Louise and Wally went to pick them up. Nate had gone separately to set up the table in the shade outside the theater. He'd already taken the baked goods that Wally had made. Orli pointed out the rest of the baked contributions to Wally, who loaded them into Louise's trunk.

Nate wasn't there when they arrived, but he had been as good as his word and the table was in place, with a note that he'd put Wally's goodies inside the theater coatroom to keep cool. Orli and Biddy got to work laying out everything, and Tillie went off to find chairs for everyone. She came back a few minutes later and told Wally and Louise where to go get them.

When she returned with the chairs, Wally found the table covered with a large checkered cloth she recognized as Tillie's from when she still had her house. It had been in one of the many boxes moved into Wally and Nate's basement for storage after Tillie moved to the senior citizen building. Wally was amazed that Nate had been able to find it.

Tillie sat at one end of the table, near a pile of paper napkins and cups. A decision had been made not to offer hot beverages, not on an evening like this, and there were two huge plastic cans, lined with plastic bags and filled with ice, for the soda, juice and water.

Biddy and Orli sat with the baked goods, ready to compute each person's purchases and issue a ticket that they would show Tillie. It was all very well organized and Wally itched to leave the women to it before she got roped into helping more.

She turned to Louise to suggest they go inside but discovered Louise missing. She was about to go find her when Tillie shrieked.

"I don't have the money!"

Biddy's head came up. "What do you mean? You need the money to make change!"

"I must have left it home!" Tillie cried. "What are we

59

going to do?"

Wally looked in her purse to see if she had enough to use as seed money for the cash box. Her wallet was woefully devoid of cash, but she had her ATM card and she promised to fix the problem.

The closest bank was right around the corner and she rushed inside the ATM booth, got some twenties, then ran into the bank to get them turned into change. There was a long line and she fretted the whole time, worrying about what was going on at the theater in her absence. Finally she got a pile of tens, fives and ones, and hurried back to Tillie.

"Oh, Wally," said Tillie, "there you are. I wondered where you went."

"I went to get you money so you could make change."

"Didn't you know? I found it in my bag. It was in a different pocket."

Wally was relieved. Aggravated, but relieved. Pushing aside her annoyance over wasting time at the bank, she went inside to find Louise.

It took a minute for her eyes to adjust to the diminished light inside. When they had, Wally found the lobby empty. It didn't make sense that Louise would have gone into the theater, though, since they had assigned seats near the front and there was no need to save a place. Tillie and gang also had assigned seats, but further back, so they could slip in after the sale but before the curtain rose.

Louise wasn't in there either. Following her hunch, Wally went upstairs to the dressing rooms and found her friend fluttering around, offering to help in any way she could.

#

The lights had flashed once and the theater was filling up when Wally went to her seat. Tillie gave her a thumbs-up and a big smile from the back of the theater, letting Wally know that the sale went well.

Nate wasn't in his seat yet, and neither was Norman,

so Wally went outside to wait for them. People streamed by on their way inside. Wally caught snippets of conversation, some pro, some con, about the new building. Likewise, there were pros and cons expressed about everything from the lack of parking to the plethora of places to eat nearby.

Still there was no Nate. Norman showed up, apologizing to Wally. "There's no need to apologize to me," she said. "Your wife is the one who will comp--"

"I know. I was rehearsing." He gave Wally a hug. "Coming?"

"I'm waiting for Nate."

"It's late."

Wally ground her teeth. "I know."

"Come inside," Norman said. "He'll be here any minute. He'd end up having to wait for you."

Wally had to agree. Nate could walk way faster than she could, especially with his long legs. She went in with Norman.

They got into their seats just seconds before Nate came down the aisle. "Where were you?" Wally asked, more relieved that he'd made it than annoyed that he was almost late.

He gave her a quick kiss. "I'll be right back."

Wally felt a tap on her shoulder and turned to find her neighbors, Barbara and Jay Fine. She chatted with them for a few minutes before Nate came back to his seat.

Norman looked at the empty seat beside him, then wide-eyed, at Wally. "She's not going on, is she?"

"I don't know," Wally said, just as Doug Norton, the spokesperson for the Grosvenor Community Theatre came onto the stage.

There was polite applause. Doug said a few words about the troupe and the trials and tribulations of the show, breathlessly and very fast. His whole explanation took less than a minute. Wally had never seen him so keyed up and hoped that wasn't a sign that he was too nervous to play his role as Mr. Peters.

Louise still hadn't taken her seat when the lights went down again.

"She's going to hate missing this," Norman said.

Wally shook her head. "She's probably watching from the wing."

A hush fell over the audience as the curtains parted, revealing a drawing room. Wally knew it well, since she had worked, albeit reluctantly at first, for weeks as part of the set design team. But something was wrong. The furniture was in the wrong place, in fact, the wing chair was missing, and there was a big hole the size of a trap door in the middle of the floor.

Hillary Parker, in the role of the maid, came onstage for her opening line to a burst of applause. She turned to the audience with a big smile, pulled out the edges of her short skirt, and gave a tiny curtsey. Before she could open her mouth, though, she spotted the hole in the floor. Her smile faded and she looked around, as if uncertain what to do. Then her eyes widened and she screamed.

The missing chair was rising on its own, coming up through the trap door on the mechanism for the upcoming magic show. When the seat cleared the stage, the audience seated in house left could see why Hillary was in such distress. On the chair was Wade Fuller, but the gash across his throat and the blood covering his chest left no doubt in anyone's mind that he wasn't just playing dead.

Chapter Eight

A collective gasp filled the audience as cast and crew members poured from the wings onto the stage to see what was wrong. Cell phones, all turned off for the performance, serenaded the horrified spectators while they were hurriedly turned on to call for help. Someone called for a doctor and five people rushed forward. As the curtain was hastily closed, someone behind Wally mumbled that if they'd called for a lawyer, half the audience would have come forward.

Norman rushed backstage. Wally and Nate were right behind. All three had one thought, Wally was sure. They hadn't seen Louise. Where could she possibly be at a time like this? Was she is trouble?

Wally trailed after Nate and Norman who ran off into the wings, each checking a side. On stage, there was bedlam. Lance was literally pulling at his hair and Courtney was fanning herself with a prop. Two young women cast members were crying and the young men were standing grim-faced. Paul and Casey Clark, the couple who played Terrance and Emily, were holding each other. Darby and Nanette Granger had held each other as they climbed up the stage-right steps and stood stricken, watching what they had helped produce turn to tragedy. Nanette was particularly pale. Wally signaled to Tillie, who knew the elderly couple, to take them to a couple of seats. She didn't want to see any more tragedy.

Several people stood around the body, but it was clear

there was nothing to be done. Wally recognized a few of them and knew they were doctors. But within a few seconds, police started arriving and clearing the area. Another minute later, Dominique Scott and her partner, Ryan Devlin, came into the mayhem.

By then Lance was taking swigs from the bottle Doug Norton kept in his vest pocket. Wally had thought it was just a prop, but it was clear Doug had filled it.

"Where is Louise?" Wally asked Lance. It had been several minutes and neither Nate nor Norman had returned.

He looked around, then back at Wally. His eyes widened and he handed the flask back to Doug. "Let's go find her," Lance said.

#

Dominique just caught a glimpse of Wally as she and some man went running from the stage. She had no time to wonder why because it was clear she, and every other police officer in the theater, would have enough to do just to sort out what was going on. One thing was certain; there had been a murder in Grosvenor, seemingly right in front of hundreds of people. With an inward groan at the sheer numbers of eyewitness accounts she would have to take, she got to work. Her first task was to contain the spectators in the theater and make sure they didn't compromise any of the evidence.

"Everyone," she said, as loudly as she could. "Please, may I have your attention?" There was barely any less of a din than before she opened her mouth. She tried again, without any success.

Ryan put his fingers to his lips and issued such a loud whistle that the entire audience immediately quieted. Dominique gave him a grateful smile. "Will everyone please take a seat?"

That done, Dominique slipped back behind the curtain. The little group of doctors who had rushed to Wade Fuller's side all looked up. One stepped over to Dominique and asked if this would take long. She figured she might as well start with him.

"The victim's throat was slit," he reported, after giving his name and address. He seemed quite upset. "I'd say he died just a few minutes before he was discovered. If we'd only known he was down there, we might have been able to save him."

"Doubtful," said another of the doctors. "Whoever did this severed both carotid arteries. Exsanguination would have been almost immediate."

Dominique finished with the doctors as quickly as possible. She might not have known for sure how long ago Mr. Fuller had been attacked, or whether he could have been saved if he had been found sooner, since opinions varied, but she had a clear picture of what had happened medically to the victim and a statement from each physician. She really wanted to talk to the cast members, hoping one of them, at least, had seen something.

Courtney Haven, whom Dominique recognized from an old soap opera that her grandmother had loved, sat on one of the chairs in the stage living room. Dominique asked her to explain her role in the play.

She was dressed in what might pass for vintage Chanel. "My cue was coming up. I was going to make my big entrance into the drawing room."

"What happened?"

"Hillary, she's the one who is wearing the French maid's outfit, made her entrance. Instead of her line, all I heard was a scream. I barely had time to see if my cue would come, before people started onto the stage. So I joined them and saw--" She broke off, and wobbled.

A man came up behind Courtney to steady her. "I'm okay," she said. She put the back of her hand to her forehead. "It's so awful."

The man looked at Courtney for a long moment, then turned to Dominique and introduced himself as Doug

Norton. He handed her a playbill. "This could help you keep the actors straight," he suggested. "And in answer to your question, my character does not come on until scene two, so I was in my dressing room until I heard the commotion."

Dominique noted what he said and stole a glance at Ryan. He, and the other detectives in town, everyone having been called in on the case, was also knee-deep in witnesses. It was going to be a long night. She hoped Wally would be back soon, to help sort things out from an insider's point of view.

#

Wally hurried behind Lance as he went back toward the dressing rooms. "When I last saw Louise she was helping Courtney with her make-up" he said. "She really is such a trouper."

She might be a trouper, Wally thought, but she was missing and with each passing second Wally became more frightened.

No one was in the dressing area. Wally ran downstairs. Once down there she found Nate and Norman, standing still in confusion.

"You think she's down here?" Lance asked from behind Wally. "There's really no place—wait, follow me."

All four of them ran into area beneath the stage. A set of steps on wheels stood off-center from the trap-door opening and the magician's lift mechanism, apparently assembled early, stood beneath the open trap door. The lights from over the stage shone around the edges of the lift.

Several prop closets lined the far wall of the cavernous basement. Wally knew they were all empty, since the theater was brand new. But it seemed they were the only other place Louise could be. As Wally hurried over to check them out, a muffled sound came from one of the enclosures. "Nate," Wally called, picking up her pace.

"Louise?" she said, as loudly as she could.

There was a thumping on a door and everyone raced over to it.

"Let me out!" Louise voice sounded frantic.

"Someone find a key," Norman shouted. "We've got to get her out of there."

"Maybe it isn't locked," Wally said. She opened the door to find Louise, with duct-taped hands and feet, inside. Her silk scarf, which was looped around her neck, looked wet, as if it had been in her mouth. She must have somehow worked it loose.

Norman helped her to her feet as Nate and Lance worked to unbind her legs. The new shoes Louise had bought for the occasion were scuffed beyond redemption, Wally noted, probably from using them to kick the door.

Wally ruined her new manicure getting the tape off Louise's wrists. She didn't care; she just had to free her friend.

"What happened?" Norman asked his wife.

"I don't know. Someone hit me from behind and I saw stars, literally. I always thought that was just a saying."

Norman nodded impatiently. "Go on."

"When I came to, I was in the dark, bound and gagged." She took her scarf off, looked at it in disgust, and threw it on the floor.

"We have to get you to the hospital," Norman said, examining her head. "Right now." He helped her toward the stairs. "There is probably an EMT and ambulance outside."

Louise pulled away from her husband's arms. "Why? What's going on?"

"Wade Fuller was found, murdered," Wally said, hardly believing it. Suddenly it felt very cold in the basement. "His body was on the wing chair. It came up through the trap door on the lift."

Louise's mouth hung open but only for a moment.

"Do you think whoever did that was the person who put me into the closet?"

Norman swallowed. "It seems likely. Please, let's just go upstairs."

"Bring the duct tape," said Wally. "And be careful with it. Maybe there will be some fingerprints, if we didn't ruin them getting Louise loose."

Nate's face was ashen. "This is way too close to home. You aren't going to get involved in this, are you?"

Wally didn't see how she could avoid it, but she didn't think that was what her husband wanted to hear. "I'll try not to," she said.

That answer did not seem to satisfy Nate. But it would have to do.

When they returned to the stage, Tillie rushed over to make sure they were all okay. Norman went to look more closely at the bump on Louise's head and Lance to talk to Dominique. Wally and Nate were left, for the moment, to deal with his mother. "We're okay," Wally said. "What about the others?"

Tillie tilted her head toward the back of the theater, where Biddy sat openly eating popcorn and Orli stood talking the ears off the Grangers. "I couldn't stop her from eating in here. She asked who was going to care now?"

"That seems somewhat callous," said Wally.

"That's just Biddy. And she sold all the other snacks. People seemed to think they were going to be here for a long time and they were afraid they'd starve."

Wally suddenly realized that she was hungry. And she knew that if she was, Nate definitely was, since his metabolism was so much faster than hers. She wondered if he should go see if maybe Biddy had any more of that popcorn. But when she turned to him to suggest it, he was nowhere in sight.

She told Tillie she would come back as soon as possible.

"Don't hurry," Tillie said. "We can take care of ourselves. And I'll keep an eye on Nanette and Darby. They're getting up in years, you know. Besides, you're needed up there on the stage with the detectives."

Wally rolled her eyes at her mother-in-law's implication. "I'm just checking on Louise," she told Tillie.

A happy nod was the only response.

Hurrying up to the front of the auditorium, Wally went up onto the stage by way of the left wing. She found Louise at the center of a group of detectives, with Norman firmly by her side. The duct tape had been placed into what Wally figured was an evidence bag.

"Can you start again, Mrs. Fisch?" Ryan asked.

"Let me sit down," she said, looking around for a seat. The body was still on the chair, although it was covered, and Louise shuddered.

Lance brought her a folding chair from backstage. He also handed her a bottle of water, and opened it for her when she had trouble with the top.

"I still don't understand what was going on," Louise said. She looked up at Wally, who had gone to stand nearby.

Wally could only shrug her shoulders.

"Please, Mrs. Fisch," Dominique said. "It would be better if you tell us what you saw, before we tell you anything else. We don't want to influence your recollection."

"Okay, but I really didn't see much of anything. Mostly I heard things."

Ryan stood poised with this pencil and pad. "Such as?"

"I got a call from Babbette about fifteen minutes before we were supposed to raise the curtain. Her babysitter had been late and she was having trouble finding a parking space. She said I had to go downstairs, open the trap door, and send the chair she'd left on the lift back up through the door. Then I was supposed to push the chair into position, go downstairs again and lower the lift and close the trap door so no one would fall through. I didn't know why the chair was on the lift in the first place, since the lift doesn't have anything to do with this show. It's for the magician next Sunday."

"What did you find when you went downstairs?"

Louise thought for a moment. "I used the steps to climb up to the trap door and leaned over to open it. Then I climbed down and started to push the button to send it back up."

"But you didn't come back up," said Norman, still showing signs of stress. "We had to go find you."

"And the chair on the lift didn't come up until after the curtain was raised," said Hillary, who was still wearing her French maid's uniform. She was being comforted by Jamal. It seemed somehow wrong to Wally, since they were not a couple in the play. But that was a play, and this was real life, which couldn't get any more real.

"No," said Louise. "Someone hit me on the head. I guess." She rubbed the spot.

Norman looked at Dominique. "Can't we do this later? She should have her head examined."

Louise glanced up at her husband and smiled. "You've been saying that for years. Five more minutes won't make a difference."

There were several chuckles among the onlookers, and Wally let out some of the breath she hadn't realized she'd been holding.

"The closet where you were found," Ryan said, "was on the other side of the lower level, far from the center of the stage. How did you get there?"

"If she had been in the area of the trap door to start with and that's all she remembers," Lance said, speaking up for the first time, "she must have been dragged while she was unconscious." He turned back to Louise. "You poor darling." He looked around as if embarrassed. "Well, you know what I mean."

Dominique tilted her head. "Are you saying none of you spent any time looking at the lift or the stairs to the trap door during the search?"

"No," Wally said. "It's out in the open, and we could see that Louise wasn't there. That's why we were checking the prop closets."

Norman and Lance nodded. Nate, who was standing to Wally's right, nodded too.

He was taking this hard, Wally noticed. He looked anxious, and his usually healthy coloring was off. Wally hoped it wouldn't be much longer before they could get Louise out of there to make sure she was okay. Obviously her ordeal was getting to everyone if Nate, who was usually the picture of calm in the face of adversity, was worried about her.

An officer brought an evidence bag up to Dominique and she looked inside. He whispered something in her ear.

"Mrs. Fisch," she said, "I wonder if you can help us identify something."

Louise stood up and came over to Dominique. "I guess."

"We found these underneath the stairs to the trap door. Do you know whose they are?" As she said that she pulled a pair of sunglasses out of the evidence bag.

"No."

But Wally knew. She could clearly see where the puppy had chewed the ear piece. The sunglasses belonged to Nate.

Chapter Nine

Dominique turned toward the sound of screams coming from the lobby of the theater. Wondering what new problem she had on her hands she left the stage and hurried toward the back of the auditorium.

After some effort and a lot of elbowing her way through the crowd, she came upon the source of the noise. Surrounded by dozens of people all trying to offer assistance was Marcella Fuller, the wife of the murder victim.

A bystander quickly brought a chair for her. Dr. Brody, the man who had examined Wade Fuller, was helping her onto it as Marcella's head lolled forward. The doctor had her put her head between her legs. He knelt beside her, offering words of comfort while taking her pulse.

He stood up. "She'll be okay, but she's had a terrible shock. She should really be taken home." He turned toward Dominique. "This would not be a good time to talk to her."

Dominique was puzzled. Why had it taken a half hour for Mrs. Fuller to have her reaction to the news of her husband's death? The team from the county prosecutor's office was already there and news vans were parked just outside the theater's doors, yet the wife of the victim had only just heard of the murder. It didn't make sense.

"She can go home," Dominique said, "but first I have two questions. And we need some privacy."

Leaning heavily on the arm of Dr. Brody, Mrs. Fuller was led into the box office and given another chair. She sat head down, clutching at a quickly disintegrating tissue.

Dr. Brody stationed himself just outside the door. Dominique sat beside the new widow on another chair and offered her some tissues from a box nearby. "I would like to know where you were an hour ago.

Mrs. Fuller looked up. "I was at home."

"Alone?"

"Yes. Just like I've been every night for the past five years. The life of the wife of a restaurateur is not a glamorous one."

"Was anyone with you?"

"No."

"How did you hear--?"

The doctor opened the door and cut Dominique off as Mrs. Fuller began to weep loudly. "Marcella should be taken home." He turned to her. "Is there someone we can call?"

"Please call my daughter, Devin. She is a student at St. Michael's."

Dominique took out her cell phone and asked the desk sergeant to please find Devin Fuller at the university.

"Not Fuller," said Mrs. Fuller. "Her last name is Allen. Devin Allen. Wade was not her father." She grabbed another tissue and blew her nose before opening her purse and taking out her cell phone. "Speed dial three."

Dominique opened the box office door and signaled to a uniformed officer. "Please call her daughter and pick her up, if necessary. Make sure Mrs. Fuller gets home." Dominique hated to have to put off further questioning, but she had no choice.

"I'll take Marcella home," said Dr. Brody. "And I'll stay until Devin gets there." He helped Mrs. Fuller to her feet and out of the small office. Dominique could only watch them go.

Returning to the theater, Dominique sought out Ryan for an update. "We've talked to everyone on the stage and handed out questionnaires to the people in the audience. We'll be collecting them and screening them for the next half hour or so. Anyone with anything promising will be asked to stay, but the rest can be sent home. And the press would like a statement."

"No surprise there," said Dominique. She looked at all the people still in the theater. "There are so many questions to ask."

"True," said her partner. "Mostly, though, I think we'll be concentrating on the cast and crew."

"And Wally," said Dominique.

Ryan gave her a slow grin. "Of course."

Dominique was pleased and a bit surprised. In the past Ryan had seemed to resent Wally Morris's help. She had been the one to solve several murders, making the local and county police seem to be ineffectual. Ryan had taken it personally. Dominique smiled at her partner. "Really? You aren't going to fight it anymore?"

He sighed. "If you can't beat 'em ..."

\#

Wally looked helplessly over at Louise who was gingerly touching her head. "There's a huge bump here," she said. "And I'm getting a headache like you wouldn't believe. Does anyone have some aspirin?"

"I'll get them," Lance said. "Just hold on." He started for the little cubicle in the theater office that he'd been granted while he was directing the play. He seemed happy there was something he could do to lend a hand. There was nothing he could do about the show coming to a crashing halt, Wally knew, or the potential producers he'd invited to impress who would now never see his work, but he could help a woman who had treated him with utmost admiration for his craft, something he'd been craving for some time. Wally had to give him credit.

74

"Oh, no" said Norman. "You aren't taking anything until we get you to the hospital. They'll decide what, if anything, you can take." He helped Louise to the stage wing and started down the stairs. "Are you coming too?" he asked Wally.

Wally was startled. Her mind had gone back to Nate's glasses, so weirdly found under the trap door opening. "Um, no, I don't think…"

"May I come with you?" Lance asked.

Norman turned a puzzled face toward him. "Why?"

"Because I'm worried about her."

Louise beckoned her husband to come closer. "Let him, Norman," she said. "If he wants to."

Norman shrugged and Lance hurried to take Louise's other hand and help her. One stern look and throat clearing from her husband had him toss that idea. He walked behind them.

Wally caught his eye. He ran over to her. "I know it's strange, and I can't explain why I feel this way, but after all the cranky self-centered actresses I've met, she is like a breath of fresh air." He turned to see her exiting the theater and smiled at Wally. "She would have made a great diva." Then he turned and ran after the Fisches.

"What the heck is he doing?" Courtney said, as if she couldn't believe her eyes. Nobody answered her so she continued, explaining to no one in particular her dismay. "What a sycophant!" She looked around. Jamal was looking at her, so she went on. "Lance was actually bowing and scraping to that insipid Louise Nobody Fisch over a little bump on the head? Has he no pride?"

Jamal turned away. "Maybe it's some kind of Oedipus complex," Courtney posited, drawing Wally's ire. Louise probably wasn't even fifteen years older than Lance. But she wasn't going to get into it with Courtney, who was still complaining.

"He should be here holding his real leading lady's hand, making sure I'm okay. After all, the shock, the terrible shock, of having my big comeback stopped like that could make me too nervous to ever perform again, what with worrying that another problem would arise when I next star in a production. I might even need therapy!"

Wally was willing to bet that was probably Courtney's best acting job ever. And it wasn't over, even though she was embarrassing herself beyond belief.

"It's such a shame that the show can't go on. Lance told me he'd invited several producers to come see the play. He was hoping it would lead to more work. They could have also seen my performance and they might have realized I'd be just right for an off-Broadway show."

No one seemed to agree with her. They were looking away, and if they felt as Wally did, they were wishing Courtney would stop talking.

She did. She began to cry. No one could really blame her, for that, at least. Her big chance was blown and she didn't know when she'd have another.

"Oh, you poor dear," said Doug, after stowing his flask in the pocket of his jacket. "You are taking this so hard. Did you know Wade personally?"

He went over to Courtney and wrapped his arms around her, which looked like just about the last thing she wanted. Louise had mentioned that Doug groped Courtney every chance he got during rehearsal, particularly during the one scene at the end where they got together.

It appeared to take Courtney a moment to remember who Wade was. She looked over Doug's shoulder at the covered body on the chair, the reason for the end to her big plans, and sobbed harder.

Jamal rolled his eyes.

#

Wally was sweating under the hot lights on the stage. She and Nate stood awkwardly, dumbfounded, waiting for

76

Dominique to come back so they could talk to her.

All their years of marriage had led to a special means of communication, which came into use when they saw the chewed sunglasses that had been found under the trap door. Neither looked at the other or said a word because just as they were about to Dominique had to leave to handle someone screaming in the lobby. Talking to anyone else was unthinkable.

Nate was the first to speak. "I don't know how they got there," he said in a whisper. "I left them in the car."

"Which you left unlocked, no doubt," Wally whispered back.

"Only while I was unloading that stuff for Tillie." He frowned. "It couldn't have been more than five minutes."

"But you didn't miss them when you got back to the car?"

Nate didn't answer immediately. Something seemed to be going through his mind. Wally couldn't imagine what it was since she had no idea where Nate went after he dropped off everything.

"I guess not," he said. "I guess I would have realized they were missing eventually."

Wally craned her neck toward the back of the theater. "We have to tell Dominique right away. Do you think we should go looking for her?"

"No. Whoever was doing all that screaming sounded more important, at least for the moment."

"How can you say that? Your sunglasses might implicate you in Wade's murder."

Nate looked at her in surprise. "Are you saying you think I had something to do with it?"

"Of course not. But it's kind of creepy that your sunglasses might have. What if the killer stole them out of your car while you were delivering the table and food? What if he," Wally paused, thinking, then added, "or she wore them to disguise himself or herself and slipped into

77

the theater?"

"Maybe," said Nate. "I guess that's possible. The police can figure that out."

"Yes, but until they do, they might have a few questions for you."

Nate's face paled.

#

Dominique came back into the theater and went toward the stage. A majority of the people who had comprised the audience had been allowed to leave the theater after filling out the forms that would allow the police to be able to reach them. But the cast and crew and their families were all still standing on stage or sitting in the first rows of seats.

Most people were talking to one another in groups but Dominique noticed that Wally and Nate Morris were by themselves in a corner. She went over to them to see if they'd heard an update about Mrs. Fisch's head injury.

"No," said Wally. "But there is something we have to tell you."

"Can it wait? I have to try and figure out the timetable of events leading up to the discovery of the body. There is an awful lot to do. Maybe we can catch up later?"

Wally shook her head. "Please, it's important."

Dominique could see the concern in their eyes. "Come sit over here," she said, leading them to the side row of seats. When they were seated she looked at each of them. "What's wrong?"

Nate cleared his throat. "Those sunglasses are mine."

"How can that be?" Dominique asked. "I thought you didn't go into that area when you were searching for Mrs. Fisch."

"I didn't."

"Then how did they get there?" asked Ryan, who had apparently come up behind her. His tone was harsh.

Dominique resisted the urge to whirl around and tell him to stay out of it. Yet looking at her friends, Nate and

78

Wally, she suspected, deep in her gut, that there was no staying out of it, for any of them.

Chapter Ten

Wally felt a strange emptiness in her stomach and it wasn't just because she had missed dinner. Something was wrong, something big. The out-of-kilter sensation of having made a mistake somehow persisted for the rest of the night.

Dominique had taken a brief statement from Wally and Nate about the sunglasses and sent them home. "Don't discuss this with anyone," she cautioned. "We'll talk more about it tomorrow."

They walked out of the theater in silence. Tillie and her friends were nowhere to be seen and Wally figured they'd gone home. She hoped they'd gotten a ride.

"Do you want to call and make sure they got home?" Wally asked.

"Who?"

"Your mother and her friends."

"Okay." He took out his phone and made a one-second call. "I'll talk to you tomorrow, Mom," he promised before he disconnected the call. "They're fine."

"What are you going to tell her?" Wally asked as they reached the parking lot. They would have to drive home separately because they had driven separately to the theater.

Nate didn't answer Wally's question, he just shrugged and got into his car.

Wally, who had no parking karma at all, was parked at the far end of the lot. "Need a lift?" Nate asked, as he slowly drove past her.

Ordinarily that would have been said with a touch of humor, Wally reflected, and she would have jumped into Nate's car like a teenager going for a very short spin. But Nate's tone had been more grim than grin.

She waved him on. She needed time to think.

Wally was still searching for the words to open the conversation when she got home. The ringing phone gave her a reprieve.

It occurred to her at the last second before she said hello that it might be someone asking questions or worse, especially at that hour, calling with more bad news. She almost let it ring. But knowing Nate would get it even if she didn't, Wally took a chance.

"Hi,' said Norman. "I thought you might like an update."

Wally was relieved to hear his voice, which was relaxed, almost happy. "Is she okay?"

"I'll let you decide for yourself. We're hungry. Meet us at the diner?"

"Um," Wally stalled, wondering if it was a good idea.

Nate came into the kitchen and raised as eyebrow. "Hold on," Wally said. She covered the phone and explained the call to Nate.

His face lit up. "Tell him we'll be right there."

Louise was holding a bag of ice on her head when they got to the diner. "How did you get out of the emergency room so fast?" Wally asked. "You were knocked out. Don't they have to observe you or something?"

"They'll have to observe me later," Louise said. "I got let out to get some food while they decide what all the results of my tests were. I convinced them it would be worse for my health to not eat than to walk around. They want me to stay awake anyway."

Norman smiled. "I haven't pulled an all-nighter since college. This will be fun. Who's in?"

Wally became aware that she was scowling when

Norman laughed. "I'm not serious. You don't have to stay up with us."

"Let's order," said Louise. "What's everyone having?"

At midnight there weren't too many people in the diner with them. But the few people who were at the nearby tables seemed to be having breakfast. That appealed to Wally, especially since she was hoping to miss breakfast the next time it came around. She was looking forward to sleeping late.

Too bad her appetite, when her pancakes arrived, wasn't up to what she had ordered. Her mind worked overtime, teeming with questions for Nate that she couldn't ask at present. Just trying to keep them from popping out of her mouth as she chatted with Louise was an effort.

Luckily no one seemed to notice.

It was after one when they got home. Norman and Louise had dutifully gone back to the hospital as they'd promised the doctor, leaving Wally alone with Nate at last.

"Nate," she said, as they took Sammy out for a last minute break, "you have to tell me what's going on."

"With what?"

"With you."

He turned toward her. In the light from the porch she could see his eyes. They looked sad or maybe worried. It was just about how she felt.

"Is this about my sunglasses being found under the trap door? Are you saying you think I had something to do with Wade's murder?" He called the dog toward him and they went into the house for Sammy's bedtime treat.

Wally counted to ten and went inside after him. "Of course I don't think you had anything to do with the murder. I'm your wife and I trust you completely. I'm sure you have an explanation for everything you've been doing today. But I want to know about the other thing."

Nate wasn't in the kitchen. She was talking to the dog,

who was licking up the last crumbs of his biscuit. She got the expected answer. Silence. Sammy had nothing to say.

"Nate," she tried again, when she got upstairs. "We have to talk. It's not the sunglasses, not about Wade. I know you had nothing to do with that. But you weren't in your seat until the curtain went up and there might be questions."

"What are you saying?"

"It's about you disappearing all the time." She looked him right in his blue-green eyes. "What is going on?"

There was worry in those eyes when he looked back at her. "I can't tell you, specifically, and I'm sure if you knew what it was and who was involved you'd say you'd rather not know. In hypothetical terms, are you familiar with the concept of commingling?"

"Yes, it's when a person uses money, client's money, from an escrow account, for personal use. It's illegal. I know you wouldn't do that. Who did?"

Nate frowned. "I was talking hypothetically."

"Right." She put up her hand. "You know? You were right. I don't want to know who did that."

"I'm sure it will all be over in a few days."

"How are you going to fix it? And why?"

"I'm working on it. Let's just leave it at that. And because I can't throw this guy to the wolves. It was an accident, but he doesn't need the headache of trying to prove that at this time."

His tone left no room for 'maybe we'll talk more about it.' Wally wondered how she could stand waiting for it to be over.

#

"Thanks for coming," Dominique said to Wally when she arrived at the performing arts center at noon. "We need your help. We don't have much to go on."

Wally shuddered. As far as she knew, the only hard evidence they had was a pair of Nate's sunglasses. She knew he was not the one who killed Wade, but would the investigating detectives accept her word on it? "I was afraid of that."

Dominique sighed. "You have to relax," she said. "Nobody thinks Nate had anything to do with the murder. We're checking the sunglasses for fingerprints. If we get lucky, this whole thing could be over soon."

Wally certainly hoped so. But after a sleepless night she wasn't really capable of believing it. And since she and Nate had missed going to Shabbat services since they'd slept so late, she felt even more out of whack. Things just didn't seem right, somehow.

"Okay, then," said Dominique. "What I was hoping you'd do is walk me through the way the play was supposed to go forward and see what, if anything, seems out of place."

Looking at the stage from in front of the first row of seats only made Wally feel worse. It had all looked so good just yesterday afternoon. "For one thing, the chair didn't belong in the center of the stage. It belonged against that wall." She pointed. "I really don't know who put it onto the trap door, or when."

Dominique noted that. "It's among the questions we're asking everyone. What else?"

Wally walked up onto the stage. Everything else was just like it was yesterday afternoon. "I don't see anything else out of place, I don't think."

She turned toward Dominique. "I'm sorry."

"Don't worry about it. It was a long shot. But maybe you could direct me to who would know about the placement of props?"

"You are looking at one of those people. However, the person in charge is Babbette Fay. Have you talked to her?"

Dominique pulled out a list of the cast and crew and looked up Babbette's number. She took out her cell phone and placed a call. After explaining who she was and advising Babbette that she would still be responsible for filling out a detailed statement, Dominique asked her if she knew how the chair got to the middle of the stage.

She was silent, listening, asking a few more questions, then she thanked Babbette and ended the call. "She says she was the one who put it there," said Dominique. "She sounded very upset."

"Why did she move it?"

"Someone had spilled something on it," Dominique said. "Mrs. Fay was trying to get it out with cleaning fluid and was worried that the fumes, combined with the new carpet odors of the theater, would nauseate people. So Mrs. Fay, who claims to have had experience with magician's lifts, opened the trap door and moved the chair onto the lift, then lowered it down to the basement. She finished cleaning it and left it there to dry. As Mrs. Fisch told us, Babbette had difficulty getting back to the theater, so she called asking for a favor. Babbette got to the theater a little while later, but when she went up onto the stage she saw the hole in the floor, so she rushed downstairs. By the time she got downstairs, she saw that someone had sent it back up. So she went back upstairs."

"Did she also think someone had moved the chair back into position?" Wally asked.

She realized that she'd said that a bit sharply when Dominique's head came up from reading her notes. "Yes. She thought Mrs. Fisch must have been in the middle of doing that as she asked. So, since it was so close to the curtain, she let it go."

"That means she was down under the stage after Louise was stuffed into the closet!"

"The closet was far away from there. She wouldn't have heard Mrs. Fisch even if she were conscious."

"But Babbette might have seen the murderer. Or been knocked out like Louise was," Wally said, for some reason worrying unreasonably about an event that hadn't happened. She had to get a grip. "It's just strange, that's all. From what I know of Babbette, she would have planned to be here a lot earlier than just before the play started, to be sure everything was in position."

"I'll find out why she was late, if you think it's important," said Dominique.

Wally was frustrated. She wanted more than anything to find some evidence that would implicate someone other than Nate, but she couldn't just throw out questions that might incriminate other people. She was beginning to feel as if she couldn't open her mouth about anything. If she did someone might think there was a possibility that Babbette was late for some less than above board reason.

But what was really making her want to seal her lips was whatever was going on with Nate. It was beginning to get to her. Even though his secret meetings and his efforts on behalf of a mystery acquaintance were unrelated to the murder, they added to her tension. "How should I know?" she snapped. "I don't know how any of this could have happened."

"I'm sorry," said Dominique. "I should have realized how upset you are. Why don't you go home now and if you think of something call me, but otherwise don't worry about it."

"Thanks," said Wally, before hurrying down off the stage and up the aisle to the lobby. Pushing her way through the theater doors, she went out into the sunshine. The way she felt, though, it might as well have been raining.

Chapter Eleven

Dominique looked at Inspectors Davis and Brady and waited until they were seated next to Ryan in the conference room of the Grosvenor police station. She was in charge of this investigation, maybe not officially, but in fact. It was a position she had earned after years of proving herself and her capabilities and she wasn't about to take a back seat to anyone.

Inspector Davis, who was ferret-like in both behavior and appearance, being a thin person with an abundance of nervous energy, and his laid back paunchy partner, Brady, were members of the County prosecutor's office and by rights had the responsibility for collecting the facts on the homicide. But experience in prior investigations with the two men had given Dominique enough street credibility to demand respect for her ability. She didn't expect those two men to just sit back and let her direct the investigation, but at least for the moment she was the one with all the information and all they had were a few lab reports. It was time to bring them up to speed.

"We secured the area, took down the information on everyone present inside or near the theater, got a list of all the cars in a six block radius, since the parking lot was filled to capacity, and some people had to park elsewhere, and took statements from the cast and crew." What she reported was perfectly obvious to everyone in the room, but it needed to be said. If she didn't mention the extent of the evidence gathering, Davis would find a way to make her feel inadequate.

"The victim was attacked around 7:45," she continued.

Davis, true to form, jumped on her statement. "How can you be so sure?"

"A witness was in the basement near the lift that held the wing chair. She had her hand on the switch to send it up when she was hit over the head. That was just after 7:45. Whoever hit her tied her up and threw her into a closet. If the body was already on the high backed chair, she was not aware of it. However, it could have been and she might not have seen it, as it was facing away from her."

"Wouldn't she have seen the back of his head?"

"It's possible she didn't get close enough to see over the back of the chair. If not, she would probably not have seen the victim, since he was under five-and-a-half feet tall."

"Did we get anything on the fingerprints on the lift and chair yet?"

"No. But many sets were found." Dominique looked at Davis. "Most of the people involved probably never had to have their fingerprints taken and there is a possibility that some on the lift mechanism might be from a completely different location. This could take a while."

"Who are we seeing this morning?" Brady asked, looking up from his copy of the witness list.

Ryan, who had been sitting quietly, shifted in his chair, causing it to squeak. "We are going to speak to Mrs. Fuller and her daughter, Devin."

Davis looked expectantly at Dominique. Since they would be splitting into teams, she would be paired with the senior inspector. "I'd like to start with Louise Fisch," she said. "She is a real estate agent and was very involved in the production of the play. Mrs. Fisch was the closest person, other than the victim, to the murderer and she was attacked herself."

Before they were even out of the building Davis had lit up a cigarette. Dominique shook her head. Some things never changed.

Louise Fisch had been released from the hospital at seven in the morning. Her husband seemed happy to report that aside from her after-midnight meal when she was briefly out of sight of the staff of the hospital, she had been undergoing tests and under observation for over ten hours and she was considered on the road to recovery.

Dominique found her sitting propped up on pillows on the sofa in her family room. Next to her was a land line phone, a cell phone, a remote control, a Blackberry, a laptop computer. A cup of tea and a half eaten bagel were on the coffee table beside her and a light blanket covered her legs. She seemed ready for anything. Her husband took a seat beside her. He seemed more concerned about her condition than she did.

After introductions, Dominique and Davis sat on the love seat opposite. "Mrs. Fisch," Dominique said, "could you please explain to Detective Davis what happened last night? Take it slowly. Maybe you'll remember something else."

Mrs. Fisch smiled. "Wally told me to think about it and write anything down, anything at all, that came to me."

Davis bristled. "If that Morris woman is interfering in this case we are going to have to take action."

It didn't sound as if Wally was interfering, Dominique thought, but she wished Wally's name had not come up. It was an even sorer subject to Davis and Brady than it had been to Ryan.

Mrs. Fisch looked hurt. "Are you threatening my friend?"

Mr. Fisch shook his head. "Don't worry about it." Turning to Davis, he said, "Wally wouldn't let us talk about what happened. She said you were the ones to tell."

"Now?" asked Mrs. Fisch.

"Yes, please," said Dominique.

"Okay. Well I don't think anything new came to me other than what I told you last night. I had gone up onto the stage to look around and, um…" She chewed on her lip. "This is kind of embarrassing."

"Mrs. Fisch," said Davis, "this is a murder investigation. Would you please answer the question?"

"I was imagining that I was going to be in the play after all. I wanted to stand on the stage, even if no one could see me. So I went behind the curtain and that's when I saw the hole in the floor. I didn't understand what it was right away, but then I remembered our theater tour and the way Harvey Floyd had bragged about the theater having what few other small theaters had, a way of having people disappear and reappear, using the trap door. When I figured out what the hole meant, I went downstairs to close the trap door. On the way I got a call from Babbette, telling me about the chair. When I got downstairs, I went to push the button to bring the lift up. I was going to close the trap door as soon as the chair cleared the stage, then run up to move the chair into place."

Davis turned to Dominique. "Where is the control panel in relation to the lift?"

Ms. Fisch answered for her. "It's right on the side. A switch. But I never got that far."

He looked back at Mrs. Fisch. "So you weren't right next to the lift or the couch, right?"

"Chair," she corrected. "And no. I wasn't that close. But I could see that it was on the platform. And I knew I had to send it up and then go move it." She looked over at Dominique. "I just don't know why it was down there to begin with. Babbette didn't have time to explain. But it didn't matter, it needed to go up." She pursed her lips. "Then again, I guess it did matter. Do you think the murderer killed Wade and then sent the whole thing downstairs to give himself time to get away? No, that doesn't make sense. Maybe—"

"Please let us ask the questions," growled Davis. "Tell us about your relationship with the victim, please."

"I didn't have one," Mrs. Fisch told him. "I knew who he was, what an idiot he could be, and how mean he was. But I didn't know him well." She looked at her husband. "If you want to know more, you should ask Norman. He's had dealings with Wade. Wade made you pretty angry, didn't he?"

"Gee, thanks, hon," said Mr. Fisch.

Mrs. Fisch covered her mouth with her hand for a moment. "Oh, I didn't mean that the way it sounded."

"We'll talk to Mr. Fisch when we're done with you," said Davis. "You can go now," he told Mr. Fisch. His tone was nothing short of a dismissal.

When he was gone, Dominique asked, "Mrs. Fisch, do you know anyone who might have wanted to kill Wade Fuller?"

"No. I mean I know there were people he drove crazy, but most people realized he was just a blowhard who liked to push his weight around. Norman knew how to get around him. So did Nate."

Davis looked at Dominique. "Who is Nate?"

"Mrs. Morris's husband."

"What does he have to do with this? Was he there?"

Dominique didn't say anything for a moment. She didn't want to mention the sunglasses in front of Mrs. Fisch. "He was. We will be talking to him."

Davis looked at Mrs. Fisch again, and she was beginning to redden. "I'm sure Nate didn't have anything to do with it either. Or Lance."

"Lance? Lance who?"

"The director," Louise explained. "He, and really everyone, had to put up with Wade's rules about using the theater. They changed every five minutes. It got so we thought he was going to cancel the show."

"Who else would have been affected?" Dominique asked.

Mrs. Fisch thought for a moment. "Oh, let's see.

91

Courtney Haven was worried that if the play was cancelled the big producers from New York that were invited wouldn't get to see her act. She actually threatened Nate's mother that if she and her friends kept insisting that they sell food inside the theater during the production, causing Wade to cancel the performance, she would sue them."

"Is that the same Nate?" asked Davis. He added that to his notes. "You say that Miss Haven threatened Mr. Morris's mother? And this was about something to do with the victim?"

"I'm not saying anything like that. I was talking about Courtney." She stopped, looking guilty. "But I'm sure she didn't have anything to do with it either."

"Let us figure that out," said Davis. "Ms. Scott," he continued, looking at Dominique. "I think it's time to talk to Mr. Fisch, and then you will call your friend Mrs. Morris and ask her to have her husband meet us at the station. Call Ms. Haven too. And whoever this Lance guy is. I'd like to speak to each of them before we talk to the rest of the cast."

#

"I think I did something stupid," Louise said when she called Wally.

"What did you do?"

"Well," she started, in that I'm-going-to-draw-this-story-out-to-get-the-maximum-drama-out-of-it way she had that reminded Wally of what a good actress her friend was, "I was being questioned by your friend Dominique and that guy Davis from the county."

"You were? Aren't you recovering from a head injury?"

"Oh, I am. Norman's got me set up with an entire entertainment and office center at my fingertips while I heal. He's so sweet and he's fluttering around me like a puppy."

Wally chuckled at the mixture of metaphors and tried to focus on what the problem was. "What did you tell them?"

"I told them about finding the lift down."

That didn't sound like something stupid to Wally. "So then what's the problem?"

"I accidentally mentioned Norman having dealings with Wade. So Norman had to sit and get questioned all about that by those two."

Wally knew that Louise was fond of Dominique, so she figured the problem must have been with Inspector Davis. But then again, for Dominique to be doing her job, she was likely to have some questions of her own.

That only reminded Wally of Nate's problems. And that was a subject she wasn't ready to consider right now. "I'm sure they would have asked Norman questions at some point," Wally told Louise. "After all, they did have some blowups about GrovePAC."

"Are you saying you think Norman had something to do with Wade's death?"

"No, of course not."

"Because Nate was part of those meetings. And the detectives were very interested in him. And Courtney."

Wally's head was spinning. "What are you talking about?"

"That's what I mean. I didn't even know what I was saying, but I think I might have gotten all of them in trouble."

"All?"

"I mentioned Lance, too. Now Inspector Davis and Dominique probably think one of them did it." She was beginning to sound distressed and that could not be good in her condition.

"Slow down," said Wally. "I'm sure it'll be all right. It's ridiculous to think that either Lance or Courtney would have done that. The result was exactly what they wouldn't want—a cancelled show."

Louise sniffled. "True."

"And no one would think that Norman or Nate hit you over the head and stuffed you into a closet."

"Right."

"So what are you worried about?"

"You're right, I don't know." Louise was sounding cheerier. That made Wally feel better, somehow. "Besides," Louise added, "as soon as they find out who those sunglasses belong to, they'll arrest him and the murder will be solved."

Wally's little happy bubble burst. That was the last thing she wanted to happen. And the worst part was waiting for it to be revealed. She briefly wondered if she should mention it to Louise, on the basis that if it's all so innocent they wouldn't be trying to hide it. Then again, it wasn't her secret to blab around the community. Plus, Dominique was handling it.

"Wally?" Louise's voice sounded worried. "Wally, are you still there?"

"Yes. Listen, I have to go now, but I'll be by to check on you later."

Chapter Twelve

Inspector Brady crowded his bulky body into the booth beside Dominique. Ryan and Davis sat opposite them in the Grove diner. Their conversation, once they had ordered, was limited due to the sensitivity of the case and their lack of anything else in common.

Over lunch they were able to exchange some information about their interviews with the witnesses. Ryan answered Dominique's raised eyebrow with a head shake. They hadn't learned anything from Marcella Fuller or her daughter, Devin, who had supposedly liked her latest step-father about as well as could be expected, given what they were learning of his reputation.

"We still need to know the sequence of events last night," said Dominique. "She didn't know about Wade's death until she got to the theater, apparently. What brought her there?"

Ryan looked at his notes. "She got a call from a friend of hers who was attending. All the friend told her was that she'd better get over there." He showed the name of the friend to Dominique, but she didn't recognize it. She jotted it down, planning to ask her best source of local information, Wally Morris, what she knew about the woman.

"Did you verify that call?" Davis asked.

Brady shot him a look over his ham-and-cheese club. Dominique sighed inwardly. Davis's veiled attempt to make Ryan look inadequate was spilling over onto his own partner.

"It was made one minute after the curtain opened," Ryan said.

"Did you talk to the person who made the call and ask what took so long?" Davis asked sarcastically.

Ryan failed to get the dig. "Yes. She had to wait for her phone to turn on. She had turned it off to watch the show."

Davis wiped his mouth and leaned back in the booth. "Nice friend. Setting her up for a shock."

Ryan shook his head. "She said she didn't want to tell her for fear she'd get into an accident. And she knew she couldn't go get her, since it was unlikely anyone would be allowed to leave the theater."

"All these people think they know so much about police procedure," Davis growled, "don't they?"

No one replied.

"She didn't know who else to call," Ryan added.

"If you say so."

Ryan shrugged. "Brady and I are going to track the victim's movements yesterday. We're also going to look at his books and accounts. A couple of people mentioned that Fuller was a snake in his business dealings."

Dominique hid a smile. She could see the influence of Ryan's girlfriend, Crystal, in that statement. There might be some truth to it, though, since Crystal worked the reception desk in Resplendence Salon and Spa, the most gossip filled hair salon in town. If Wally didn't have the information they needed, Dominique might just go see Crystal.

"Thanks for coming," Dominique said when Wally and Nate walked into the police station on Sunday afternoon.

"We just want to get this straightened out," said Nate. Agreeing wholeheartedly, Wally followed both of them into the conference room off the court room.

"What, no interrogation room?" Nate quipped, but there was no laughter in his eyes. From their conversations during the day, Wally could only tell that whatever the problem was that he was helping his anonymous friend with, it wasn't over yet. The issue of his sunglasses was barely a blip on the problem radar.

As soon as they were seated, Davis, with his

characteristic gruffness, asked Nate to explain just how his sunglasses had come to be on the floor next to the bottom of the lift. From what Wally remembered seeing of the vast empty floor when she was in the theater basement frantically searching for Louise, there was no place else the glasses could have been except underneath the lift when it was in the down position. Whoever had left them there must not have seen them when he or she went away.

After killing Wade Fuller. The thought made Wally shudder.

"As I explained, they were in the car when I last saw them. The car wasn't locked because I was running in and out of the theater. I don't remember seeing them after that point. But I really wasn't looking."

"Did you check to see if anything else was missing from your car?"

Wally looked at Nate in surprise. He seemed equally at a loss. "Such as?"

Davis stood up. "Did you bring the car with you?"

Nate furrowed his brows. "Yes. Why?"

"We'd like to go through it with you to see if anything else is missing. If you refuse, we can get a warrant."

Nate shook his head. "I have nothing to hide. Let's go."

Dominique led the way to the parking lot.

Nate's blue Saab was parked in a visitor space. At Davis's nod, he pushed the automatic door-lock opener and got into the driver's seat. He looked around and shrugged at Wally who was standing just outside the door.

"Nothing?"

"Not that I can see."

Wally looked in too. "Nate, did you have a hat with you?"

"I don't know. Probably."

"There isn't one in the car."

Dominique cleared her throat. "Is there something

97

missing?"

Wally looked at her. "Nate usually has a hat in the back seat. He puts it on when he goes out in the sun."

"I could have left it home," Nate said.

"Maybe." Wally didn't like the feeling she was getting, as if she and Nate had been violated. Someone had stolen his sunglasses out of his car and maybe his hat, too. Both items could have been used to help disguise whoever killed Wade.

She looked over at Dominique. "Maybe you should check the whole car."

#

"Levine," said the prosecutor on the phone on Monday morning. "My office. Now."

It was a call Elliot had been expecting. There was no way he could fly below the radar on the murder in Grosvenor—not when the police claimed to have evidence against his father-in-law, Nate Morris.

At first it had been practically nothing. Nate's sunglasses were found near the scene of the murder. Though they had no blood on them, there was a trace of blood nearby. Several police photos showed the glasses within two feet of where the body had been before the lift mechanism was activated, sending the body and the chair it was on up onto the stage in front of a sell-out crowd of 430 people. Lab tests showed no fingerprints on the glasses.

Elliot had taken that as a good sign. He had even found likely explanations for Nate's baseball cap being found in the lost items bin of the theater. A stage hand had picked it up shortly before the five minute warning for the curtain. The location of the find, however, in the back of the theater in the hallway which led to a rear fire exit, was puzzling. Nate couldn't have been there until he and Norman went in search of Louise.

But that could be explained, if one were to assume that whoever stole Nate's glasses from his unlocked car also took his cap. It could have been discarded when the perpetrator left the theater.

Armed with his suppositions and his unshakeable feeling that his wife's father could not possibly have had anything to do with Wade Fuller's murder, Elliot found his way to the prosecutor's office.

The prosecutor was not one for pleasantries. "Sit down."

Elliot sat in the left-hand chair of the two facing the prosecutor's desk. He couldn't say why he almost always chose that chair, maybe because it was closer to the door. Too much time spent in the presence of one of the most overworked prosecutors in the country tended to make Elliot want to escape.

The prosecutor tossed a file across the desk in Elliot's direction. "Tell me about Nate Morris."

"He did not commit the murder, if that's what you're asking. To think so is ridiculous." Almost immediately Elliot wished he hadn't added that last bit. If the prosecutor thought Nate could have done it, it would be as if Elliot had just called him ridiculous.

"Your loyalty is admirable. But we are dealing with facts here."

Elliot gave him his thoughts on the two pieces of evidence which had connections to Nate. An impatient finger drumming made him keep it short, but there wasn't much to say, anyway.

"Are you aware that the coroner has identified the weapon?"

"No." There had been speculation about it for days. Elliot leaned forward, hoping to hear that whatever it was would clear Nate for good. "What was it?"

"A box cutter."

A ripple passed over Elliot's skin. His father-in-law had a box cutter. Then again, so did he. It came in handy in countless household chores, especially, Elliot had learned, in wallpapering. In fact, he had put Nate's initials on his when he borrowed it so that both he and Debbie could work on the wallpaper at the same time. She was determined to re-wallpaper or strip and repaint every room in their house in an effort to make what was once his parents' house truly their own.

The prosecutor's face softened a bit, an unusual and almost frightening sign. "His initials are on it."

Elliot gulped.

"Are you okay?"

"Er, um, yes."

While wondering how the murderer could have gotten his hands on something that was in Nate's basement workshop, Elliot tried to come up with a scenario that would explain the presence of the knife. "Where was it found?"

"In a dumpster behind the Chinese restaurant."

"That's at least a hundred yards away from the theater," Elliot said. "How would the murderer have gotten that far away without being seen?"

"There was plenty of time to kill Fuller, run out the back door, throw out the knife and come back around through the front with the rest of the crowd. Morris could have done it. From what I understand, he was one of the last people into the theater."

Elliot didn't know what to say. He still refused to believe that Nate could have done it, but he knew he didn't have the evidence to prove it.

"The reason I'm telling you all of this is because this is a high profile case and because Inspector Davis is worried about interference from you and the police force in your town. Everyone seems to respect your-father-in-law and believe he had nothing to do with the murder."

"I'm sure he didn't do it," said Elliot.

"I can't ignore what I have. I think there is enough to at least look into it further."

Elliot got up to leave. "I can be in Grosvenor in twenty minutes."

The prosecutor narrowed his eyes. "Don't even think about it. I want you to stay as far away from the case as you can. It won't be yours. You are too closely tied in."

That was not an unexpected statement. But Elliot wanted to be sure that the one who did get the case would do his or her best to make sure of the facts without jumping to any conclusions. "Who is going to take it?"

"Adarra Dane."

Shaking his head, Elliot appealed to his boss. "She's so--"

"Ambitious?"

Elliot would have chosen cutthroat as a descriptor, rather than ambitious, but it amounted to the same thing.

His only hope now was for Dominique to straighten it all out before Adarra made her presence felt on the case.

#

"Have you finished getting the records?" Adarra Dane asked as she swept into the Township of Grosvenor Village police station. She was looking directly at Dominique as if no one else existed.

Dominique invited her to the little cube she shared with Ryan and introduced him to the assistant prosecutor. Ryan put out his hand but Adarra ignored it, focusing instead on sitting down expectantly in the only spare chair in the room.

She was a striking olive-skinned woman with large brown eyes and long, straight-jet-black hair cut to frame her heart-shaped face. She wore a suit that looked as if it had been made for her and high-heeled shoes that would invite any male within eyeshot to take a long look at her legs. Dominique, who was not always comfortable with her own good looks, envied the poise with which Adarra carried herself, but she knew that kind of self-assurance came with an attitude.

101

"They're here," Ryan said, hurrying to give them to this woman who in one second had taken over the cube.

Adarra took the report and read it. Dominique found herself holding her breath, hoping the obvious conclusions in the report wouldn't be so obvious to the AP.

But when she put the file down it was clear that she'd made up her mind. She looked at Dominique and said, "Is Nate Morris being held?"

Ryan stared at her. "You think Mr. Morris did it?"

Dominique held her tongue. She knew trouble was coming.

Adarra uncrossed her legs and leaned toward Ryan. "If this man is a friend of yours I want you off the case."

To his credit, Ryan did not look at Dominique. He just gave a short nod and left the room.

Wondering whether she should confess to Adarra her relationship with Nate, Dominique considered her options. She could keep the relationship to herself, risking Adarra discovering it and taking some kind of action against her, or she could report it. The latter option would cause the AP to transfer the case to someone who might not care enough to do the best job possible. Not that she doubted any of her colleagues, but Nate, Wally, and Elliot deserved someone who would look under every rock trying to find the truth.

The door to the cube opened and Ryan came back in. Chief Jaeger was right behind him. "There is no one on the force," Jaeger said, "who doesn't know the Morrises, and that includes the guys from the county. If you want everyone to start over from the beginning, tell me now and I'll assign new people. But I'll only do that if you are going to get new inspectors. I'm not going to bankrupt this department if you aren't going to take the same steps."

Adarra didn't say anything. Jaeger looked at her and said, "I thought so. Ryan, get back to your seat and help this nice prosecutor find out who killed Wade Fuller. And do it soon. I'm tired of those news vans everywhere."

#

B. J. Waters did her sound check with her cameraman and positioned herself for the live broadcast on the noon news. As a backdrop she had chosen the front of the Grosvenor Performing Arts Center. To her left, off camera, several produce vendors were setting up their booths for the farmer's market. B.J. was itching to get over there and buy some fresh vegetables, although she had no idea when she'd ever get to prepare a meal with them. Business, that is the business of reporting on criminal cases, was booming.

Grosvenor was becoming far too familiar. It was a pleasant town with well-kept large and small houses, increasingly upscale shops and it was on the train line for quick access to New York City. The community was well diversified and there was an excellent school system. It seemed an unlikely place for murder. But looks could be deceiving.

She got her cue. Reading off the paper in front of her she began her report. "I'm standing here in front of the new Grosvenor Performing Arts Center where the very first production was cut short by the death of a notable restaurateur in town." The camera light went off as the file films were aired along with the voice-over she had done earlier. A crew that was hastily dispatched to the town the night before had missed most of the people leaving the theater but had been present when the body was removed to the coroner's office.

The camera light was back on and B.J. was live again. "This untimely death in the performing arts center occurred just as Mr. Fuller was expanding his business, ironically, because of the anticipated increases in people coming to Grosvenor to attend the performing arts center. This has been B.J. Waters reporting live from Grosvenor. Back to you in the studio, Bill."

"B.J.," the news anchor asked, "do the police have any

idea who might have committed this heinous crime?"

"If they do, Bill, they aren't saying anything about it."

B.J. saw the light go off on the camera. She knew Bill was still talking to her, or pretending to, on camera for the viewing audience, advising her to keep them posted. Glad that was over, at least until five, she scurried over to buy some of those wonderful New Jersey tomatoes before they got picked over.

#

"Wally," Dominique whispered when she and a uniformed officer came to the Morrises' front door. "I'm sorry. But we have to do this."

"Is Elliot on his way?"

"Yes. We had to call him. He won't be assigned the case, but he had to know."

"Case? There is no case. Nate didn't do anything."

"I'm sure you're right. But we didn't find any odd fingerprints in Nate's car that might implicate an intruder. And the sunglasses put him at the scene."

"There were no fingerprints on the knife," Wally said. "So why would you think there would be on the sunglasses? Or in the car? Obviously the person who did this was wearing gloves." She paused, taking a breath. "Tell me that isn't the only thing you have, because it's just ridiculous."

Dominique sighed but remained silent. Wally took that as a sign that this was a losing battle, for the moment. Could there be something else?

Whatever it was, there was no way she was going to take the arrest of her husband lying down.

#

"Tell them Elliot," Wally said, her voice shaking. "Tell them there was no blood on Nate's clothing. Ask them how he managed to slit someone's throat and not get blood on himself."

Elliot looked at the woman who was his mother-in-

104

law. She was a force to be reckoned with and he tried never to be on the opposite side of an argument with her. But this was beyond his control. In his heart he knew his father-in-law was not guilty, but Elliot's training first as a detective and then as a lawyer, now assistant prosecutor, left him no doubt that the state was building a viable case. His in-laws needed to confide in him if he was to be of any help, but they were clammed up about something, he was sure. The only one talking at all was Wally, and she was just throwing out arguments to refute the evidence.

They were sitting in the waiting area of the Grosvenor police station while Nate was inside being processed. Elliot had no official standing in the case; he was there only to lend support where needed. And right now he needed to convince Wally that this wouldn't go away on its own.

"Nate needs a lawyer," he said.

"He has one," said a familiar voice.

"Debbie," Wally cried. She got up and threw her arms around her daughter. Releasing her, she stepped back. "I didn't want you to know about this. It's just some crazy mistake. Go back to work."

"I am at work, Mom," Debbie said, straightening her navy suit jacket. Her blond hair, usually loose or in a pony-tail, was in a tight knot at the back of her head and she looked ready to cross-examine everyone in the room. "I'm here to represent Dad." She looked at her husband. Elliot got a new vibe from his wife that he'd never felt before and didn't like at all. "And I'll thank you to stay away from my client's wife."

Wally turned surprised eyes toward both of them. "You two can't be serious. No, I absolutely forbid you to take opposite sides. We'll get another attorney. This town is filled with them."

"True," said Debbie. "But I have a license in this state too, and I'm going to use it to defend Dad. And until I talk to him and find out what's going on from the prosecutor's office, I don't want you talking to anyone."

"Why don't you just ask Elliot? He's standing right here and he's from the prosecutor's office, in case you forgot what your own husband does for a living."

Elliot had never heard that tone from Wally before. She was getting close to losing it. That was a scary thought, considering her inner strength. If she couldn't hold it together, how would any of them get through this? "I don't have all the facts," he said. "I really am not here as a representative of the prosecutor."

Debbie hugged her mother. "I'll take care of it Mom. And if I can't, I'll get someone who can. Don't worry." She walked over to the cage and rang the bell. "I'd like to see Mr. Morris," she said. "I'm his attorney."

Elliot watched as his wife was buzzed in. That left him once again alone with his mother-in-law, who was angry, frustrated, and seemed to be guilt ridden that she and Nate were causing problems in his marriage. He wondered what he was supposed to do now.

Chapter Thirteen

Wally jumped up when the door opened and Debbie came out. "What's going on? Are they keeping him here? They don't have to do that. He wouldn't run away. He didn't do anything."

Debbie, who had started holding her hand up as soon as Wally started talking, said, "Calm down, Mom. I'm taking care of it."

Ignoring her irritation at Debbie's placating tone, Wally looked at Elliot. She was expecting to see relief of his face, instead he saw concern. Something wasn't good about this, she suspected, but there was no time to worry about that; she wanted to see Nate. "Where is your father?" she asked Debbie.

"He has to go down to Newark to be arraigned."

"This is crazy." Wally headed for the door.

"Where are you going?" Debbie called after her.

"To Newark."

"I'll drive you," said Elliot. He looked at Debbie. "Are you coming?"

She looked back at him. "I'm going with Allen." Without waiting for a response, she went past Wally and out to the street.

By the time they got to the parking lot, Debbie was gone. "Is Allen a criminal lawyer?" Wally asked as she got into the car. She hadn't heard Debbie mention him before.

"Yes. He's good. He's been a partner for several years and he knows his way around the system."

"But Debbie works in New York. Can Allen be Nate's

lawyer in New Jersey?"

"Yes. He's from the firm's New Jersey office. I guess Debbie called him as soon as she heard that Nate had been brought here."

Elliot turned onto Grove and took a right onto Ridge. Once they got onto the highway, Wally knew, they'd be in Newark in a few minutes. A feeling of dread came over her.

"I can't believe they'd arrest Nate just because his sunglasses and hat were stolen by a murderer. It should be obvious to everyone that he didn't do it, based on that alone."

"It will be okay," Elliot said, sounding almost convincing. "Let's just get through the next few hours and see where we are."

Wally trailed behind Elliot as they went from the parking garage to the courthouse, through security and found the courtroom where Nate's case was already being discussed. Wally could see that it nearly killed Nate to be in that position. Debbie, on the other hand, looked almost defiant in her stance beside her father. The whole arraignment took less than twenty minutes. The charges were read against Nate and he pled not guilty.

#

"Nate," said Wally, as she followed him into the house. "We have to talk this through. I can't help you if I don't know what's going on."

He turned to her. It almost broke her heart to see the misery in his eyes. "I was only trying to help my mother get set up for the bake sale. Next thing I know my stuff was stolen and I end up getting arrested. How could that happen?"

"I don't know, but I know you didn't do anything wrong. It's just that there is a chunk of time missing and you don't have an explanation for it. We have to figure this out."

Nodding, Nate opened his arms. "First I need a hug."

Wally hadn't realized how much she needed one, too. As she went into his arms she felt a release of her tension and emotion so strong that tears came to her eyes. She rested her head against his chest, listening to the heart of the man she knew so well. She didn't want Nate to see her crying, so she hung on to him while she tried to get herself under control.

"Okay," she said when she was ready to face him, "sit down at the table and we'll have some tea, cookies, and a long talk." She put up the water, let Sammy out to go play in the yard, and opened a tin full of the pinwheel cookies she'd made for Jodi's next visit. It gave her another bad moment, thinking that Jodi likely wouldn't be visiting while Nate was in such trouble. Rachel would instead leave her and Charlie home with Adam while she came to lend support.

Just as she pulled out her chair to sit the phone rang. The caller ID said it was Debbie. Nate picked it up.

He only said a few words then hung up. "She's coming over."

Wally pulled a legal pad out of her school bag, grabbed a pen and got ready to write any important ideas that came to them. "We'd better hurry."

Nate ran his hand through his hair. "It all started when Fred Neimeyer came to me about his investment account because he was splitting up with Wanda. He wanted to protect his assets from Wanda and her lawyer's greedy hands."

Wally wrote "Fred, needed to sell." Looking up expectantly, she said, "And?"

"He came to see me again a few weeks later. I'd thought we were all set, but he told me he'd changed his mind and wanted to sell everything so he could pay Wanda off. But when I told him that was the worst thing he could do, considering the economy, and their daughter, Gemma's college needs in a few years, he got very upset. He told me I could handle the transactions or he'd take his business elsewhere. I told him that if he didn't like my advice, he could certainly seek another advisor."

Wally wanted Nate to hurry the story along but knew she'd have to just be quiet and listen carefully. He'd tell it the way he had to.

Nate had some of his tea and half his cookie. Wally wondered if he tasted it at all. But it seemed to relax him, which made Wally feel better as well.

"Fred got very distressed. He apologized and then he told me something that I want you to promise you will not repeat to another soul. If it has to come out, and I think it will, it will not be from either one of our mouths. Do you promise?"

In all the years she'd known Nate he had never said anything like that to her. Wally was beginning to get afraid all over again.

"I promise."

After taking a deep breath and letting it out, Nate began. "Fred was being blackmailed. Wanda wanted a much bigger settlement and she was willing to tell a secret that would end Fred's career if it got out."

"What could be so bad? Fred is a lawyer, after all. He should know how to do things legally."

"He does, of course. But he ran into a little trouble a few years ago when his office manager left and he accidentally commingled two funds. He got it all straightened out the following week."

"He's the one you're protecting? That--?"

"He's had a hard time. No one deserves what he's been getting."

Wally did not write that on her pad. She thought about the situation for a moment. "The way you explained it on Friday night, or was it Saturday morning by then?" She shook her head. "Oh, well, that doesn't matter. It doesn't sound so serious."

"Oh, but it is. There is a paper trail. He wrote his mortgage check on his clients' trust account."

"What is that?"

"It's an account for client monies due to be paid to someone else. In this case, it was money a couple had given him to hold pending an inspection on their new vacation house down the shore. People get disbarred for doing that, or at the very least in trouble with the ethics committee. Even though he paid the money back, it could cost him."

"That seems a bit short-sighted for Wanda. If he loses his practice, how could Fred pay her alimony?"

"I'm not really sure she thought ahead or if she even cared."

Wally shook her head. "Poor Fred."

Nate nodded. "Louise calls him Naysayer, doesn't she?"

"Many people do. He's, well, how should I put it? If you say something is good, such as the building of the performing arts center, he'll say it's a waste of money."

"Believe me, I know," said Nate, showing some exasperation. "That could even be why Wanda wants a divorce. But that isn't reason to destroy him."

"I agree. And I won't say a word to anyone. But what does that have to do with everything else?"

"While Fred was telling me all of this I was trying to think of a temporary solution, so that he could sort it all out. He agreed and applied for a loan, pledging half their stocks as collateral. Wanda agreed to it, since she would get some money sooner. I had the impression that she needed it for a specific purpose."

"Why didn't they just put up the house?"

"Because Wanda is planning to keep that too."

Wally didn't feel any closer to finding out what was going on and it was beginning to irritate her. But she kept her cool by eating a third cookie, something she'd sworn never to do. She didn't even berate herself—she needed the extra sustenance due to the situation.

"Go on," she encouraged.

"The loan hadn't come through when Fred came back into my office last week. He said he needed the money right away, because his brother-in-law was going to go public with Wanda's secret if Fred didn't pay her what she wanted."

"Who is his brother-in-law?"

"Wade Fuller."

Wally felt her jaw drop. She leaned forward, nearly knocking over her mug, trying to get to Nate. She was both relieved and annoyed, since it was immediately obvious that Fred was the murderer and Nate would soon be cleared.

Nate looked up at her, startled. "No, don't jump to conclusions. Fred didn't do it."

"How do you know?"

"Um, well." Nate looked like he was choosing his words, but then he smiled. "He didn't have to. He paid Wade the money."

"But you said—"

"I said he didn't get his bank loan. I lent him the money a few weeks ago, since we had enough cash in our investment account. It was lucky for him, actually. But you can be pretty sure it didn't make me happy, paying blackmail, and to that man, especially since it was coincidentally the same amount as what he paid for the liquor license he finessed from under Telly's nose."

Wally had a momentary image of Telly's nose and his giant mustache. She shook it off. "You gave him our money?"

"Yes, as a bridge loan while he sold some of his stock. It wasn't everything we had, and he paid it back, with interest, better than the account was paying. We weren't going to starve while we waited for the repayment."

"Nate," said Wally, with as little emotion as she could manage, "you gave someone who is not a relative, not even a close friend, not someone we would even enjoy going to dinner with, a loan out of our personal accounts. Why?"

"Because I thought what was happening to him wasn't fair and that he deserved a chance to clear his name before his career was ruined. I didn't see anyone else helping out, so I did it."

"Without telling me."

"I wanted to, but I never felt the time was right. You were so involved with the play and school starting up again, and I just knew you would drop everything to try to straighten it all out--"

"I wouldn't meddle--" Wally interjected.

Nate cut her off just as quickly. "Truthfully, I didn't want anyone to know. And it isn't like there is anything we can do. He has to handle it his own way." Nate looked at Wally. "I believe Fred. He may not be Mr. Personality, but he's an honest guy."

"That's quite the endorsement. And you may be right about him." Wally wondered how Nate would have felt if she'd put him in the same position and realized, as she searched for what words to say next, that Nate trusted her judgment and would not have stood in her way. Considering that, she kept quiet.

"Fred didn't do it," Nate said again. "I'm sure of it. Wade may have been blackmailing him, and the threat that he'd do it again even after he got the money did exist, but Fred didn't do it."

"How can you be so sure?"

"I, um…"

Wally gave up on waiting for him to finish his sentence. "So that's what was going on all this time? You were worried about Fred and his problems and you had to go out and meet with him so many times?"

"Yes. That's all."

Wally looked at her husband. He was telling the truth, she just knew it. "You aren't very good at this cloak and dagger secret meeting stuff, you know. I knew there was something going on."

Nate smiled. "Maybe it isn't that I'm not good at it, just that you are too smart to be fooled. I guess in some way I was counting on that. I didn't like not telling you the truth."

"Fine. But we are no closer to helping you get out of trouble than we were. The police will find out all about the money, if what you say is true and the money you lent to Fred went to Wade. It could look like he had something on you." She thought about that for a second. "Then again, the money came back. On the other hand, it could look like you were being paid to kill him."

"And I was too stupid to cover my tracks? Now *that* would be embarrassing."

Wally shook her head, sharing his amusement, but only a bit. "I'm glad to see you are feeling better. But we have a long way to go before this is over."

Nate's face took on a serious look. "I know and I'm sorry. I guess we're going to find out who our friends are."

"You could spare them this test of their loyalty and just tell the police you weren't there."

"If only it was that simple." He sighed. "I really don't know what I can do to clear my name. I can't explain where I was that evening without implicating Fred."

"Don't you think Fred should take responsibility for you? Where were you, anyway?"

"I can't tell you without getting him into trouble."

"I beg your pardon!"

"I can't tell you. You may not have to testify against me, as my wife, but you'd have to tell what you knew about Fred. So I'm not telling you. I'll have to find another way to clear my name."

114

"Did you tell that to Debbie?"

"Yes."

"She knows this whole thing already?"

"Not all of it. Even less than you. Nothing about--"

"What do you mean you didn't tell me the whole story?" said Debbie, who was standing outside on the back porch and had obviously heard Nate's last remark through the screen door. She pulled it open and swept inside, her blond hair streaming behind her, as she indignantly approached her father.

Turning to Wally, she said, "We need to be alone. We'll see you later."

Even if Nate had asked her to stay, in this case Debbie was in charge. Wally had no choice but to leave. She carefully ripped the page off the legal pad, folded it and put it into her pocket. She headed for the door to check on Sammy, then stopped and came back for the notepad. It wouldn't do for Debbie to have a chance to see the impression of Fred Naysayer's name. At least not yet. Wally was not about to let Nate get into any more trouble over that man. If she had to turn her daughter the lawyer loose on Fred, she'd do it.

Chapter Fourteen

Elliot came home to an empty house. It wasn't all that unusual since his wife worked long hours in the city and usually came home on the 8:25 train, but today he really noticed her absence. Maybe it was because of what had happened the last time he saw her, when she had looked at him as if he was the enemy. He wasn't, she had to know that. Yet because of his job at the prosecutor's office he was on the "other side" in the current matter. But Debbie just had to understand that while he had no explanation for why her father's hat, sunglasses and utility knife were found where they were, it was clear to him that someone else had used that knife to slit Wade Fuller's throat.

What he didn't understand was why there seemed to be a monetary connection to the victim. On the day before the murder, Wade Fuller had paid off a loan of $250,000. A few weeks earlier, Nate Morris had withdrawn $250,000. One day after the murder, that money had been restored to his account, paid by Fred Neimeyer, brother-in-law of the victim. There was no direct link to the Fuller money, but the suspicious coincidence was causing Adarra Dane to seek a warrant to search Nate's home and office. The thought of it, of his in-laws' home being searched, was enough to make Elliot feel sick.

A squeak from the dog crate in the corner of the kitchen snapped Elliot out of his foul mood. Saffron, his yellow lab puppy, was waiting to greet her daddy and Elliot was not going to disappoint her.

"Let's go for a walk," he said, taking the puppy out of

the crate. He hurried her to the back door and outside. She hasn't been out since noon, when the Preferred Pet person came to walk her.

When Elliot and the puppy returned home he fed her dinner. She went at it with gusto, just like the Morris dog, Sammy, did with his food. It brought Elliot's mind back to the issue with Nate. He wondered if he should check on him.

He went to the phone but before he could pick it up his cell rang. "Elliot," said Wally, "the police are here going through my house. More are in the barn."

They hadn't wasted much time getting those warrants for the house and office, Elliot thought. He searched for some comforting words to make Wally feel better. "Don't worry," he said. "I'm sure there is nothing to find."

"I know that!" she snapped. "So why do they have to look?"

"Since Nate is a suspect--"

"That's crazy! He didn't do it. This is so upsetting."

Elliot had never heard Wally so distressed. "Do you want me to talk to him?" he asked even though he knew he shouldn't.

"Good luck. Debbie has him locked in his office. She won't let me listen to what they are saying and I bet she won't let you talk to him either."

Elliot wondered if that might be true and decided it probably was. It gave him an unpleasant feeling. He and Debbie were seldom at odds and it never went well for him when they were. There was no way to fix it, at least not yet.

"Sooner or later they'll have to eat," Wally said. She sounded calmer, or maybe just tired. "I'll start dinner. How soon can you be here?"

"You want me to come there for dinner?"

"Yes. If they are going to gang up on me, I need someone else on my side."

"There is no side other than Nate's," Elliot pointed out. This conversation was getting to him. He'd never seen Wally act like this.

"I know that. It's your wife who's setting up the barriers." She was quiet for a moment during which Elliot wondered if he was supposed to have a response to that statement. But then she took a deep breath, or at least that's what it sounded like, and said, "I'm sorry. I shouldn't be putting you in that position. You have enough going against you just being a member of the prosecutor's office. But I won't hold it against you. Please come to dinner. On the best of days I feel like the odd man out, so to speak, when Debbie and Nate are together. They have that special bond, you know."

"I'll come. But first I'm going to make some calls."

"Thanks."

#

Dominique knew as soon as she saw his name on her caller ID that she was going to be in for a few awkward moments. Elliot would want some answers and he had a lot at stake.

She felt almost as troubled as she knew he was. She knew and respected Nate and Wally Morris and didn't for a minute believe that Nate would murder someone, certainly not over monetary issues, which is what Adarra Dane seemed to think.

"Hi Elliot," she said, when she answered the call. Not giving him time to even ask, she said, "We're doing a time line of Fuller's week. If there were any people who had any words, even just in passing, we are going to find them. And we are tracing the money and what the victim did with it. We're going to find out who really committed the crime. It's just a bit tricky, since Ms. Dane insists we work on proving her case against Mr. Morris."

She heard a chuckle on the other end. "Well, then," said Elliot, "there isn't much more for me to say other than how are you holding up?"

"Probably a bit better than Wally is. Although she's a rock."

"Not today, Dominique. She isn't a rock today."

Dominique's heart went out to her old partner when she heard his voice shake. This situation was getting to everyone. She struggled to maintain a level tone. "That's because she can't do anything about it. But she has to sit this one out. Until we clear Nate, at least." She hoped that would be sooner rather than later. "How's Debbie doing? I heard she is part of the team representing Nate."

"I haven't talked to her about it," said Elliot.

That didn't sound so good to Dominique, but she didn't follow up on it. "Say hi to the Morrises for me," she said. "Tell them not to worry. So far it's only circumstantial."

"Nate's knife is a little more than circumstantial." Elliot's voice was understandably tight. He was right and they both knew it.

"Look," said Dominique. "You know I can't talk to you about the case. But you can do one thing for me."

"Anything."

"Ask Wally if there is anyone she can think of who might have had something against Wade Fuller. She might be so upset that she isn't thinking about how she could actually help. But she knows a lot of what goes on in this town that never reaches the police and it might be useful."

"Yeah, that's a great idea." Elliot sounded somewhat relieved. "I'll do that."

After ending the call, Dominique rubbed her temples in an attempt to get her headache to stop, but she knew it wouldn't until she helped clear her friend, Nate Morris, from suspicion. She had to find someone else, someone who really did want Wade Fuller dead, and to that end she was viewing hours and hours of digital video taken by the surveillance cameras in the downtown area of Grosvenor.

119

Most people were not aware of their existence and they were not used to "spy" on people, just as a safety measure for the somewhat thin police force in town.

So far she had not seen anything unusual in her high speed viewing. Her eyes were teary from peering at the screen and she wanted nothing more than to put a cold compress on them and give them a rest. But there was too much at stake for her even to risk blinking.

Day turned to night and back again. She had selected one week's worth of recordings, figuring that whatever had driven someone to murder must have happened within a few days of the actual event.

Suddenly Dominique saw Wade Fuller on Depot Street two days before the murder. He seemed to be calling out to Lance Palmer. Although Dominique suspected the director was hurrying to a train, she saw him stop and turn to the restaurateur. She adjusted the sound to see if she could get a sense of what they were saying. It was spotty, but she got a good idea of the conversation.

"I want you to put an ad for my restaurant in the program," Wade said.

"Sorry," said Lance. "They've already been printed up."

"Do them over. I want my ad in the front."

Lance scowled. "I don't have any control over that, really. You should talk to someone on the committee. Maybe they'll do an insert for you. If you paid for it, you should certainly have your ad in there."

Wade didn't say anything.

"You did pay for it, didn't you? I'm afraid at this late date it might not be possible to get it printed, and if you didn't already pay it isn't really fair to make people go out of their way to do a rush order. Your ad will just have to be left out." He glanced at his watch. "Listen I've got to catch a train." Turning, Lance started to walk away.

Wade's face grew red. He grabbed Lance by the arm.

"There were people planning to sell food in my theater," Wade said. "I told them, and I'm telling you, that is not going to happen."

"It has nothing to do with me," Lance said. "And I wasn't aware that the performing arts center belonged to you."

"And you can't use the dressing rooms," Wade went on. "You can't do anything to the theater. I won't allow it."

Lance just looked at him. But he visibly tensed when Wade said, "I can still stop the show. And I will, so you'd better listen to everything I'm saying. And you'd better make sure my ad gets in."

Dominique could see that Lance had been worried. She knew, from what she had learned in her interviews at the theater, that Lance had a lot riding on the show. He'd been out of work for a long time and was using this, just like Courtney Haven was doing, as a comeback. If the show didn't go forward, it could end Lance's career.

"Look," Lance said, "I haven't done anything on your list of prohibitions. I've got to get to my train. We can talk tomorrow. Maybe something can be done about your ad."

Wade's response was drowned out by the arrival of the 3:50 Midtown Direct. Lance left him standing there and ran for it. Wade turned on his heel and went out of the range of the camera. Dominique just caught a glimpse of Lance mouthing the words, "Drop dead."

For the first time she felt she'd been thrown a life-line. Here was an example of someone who might have hated Wade Fuller enough to kill him. The man had stood in the way of the production every step of the way and had represented as big a threat to Lance's career as his reputation as an alcoholic.

She rose and stretched, getting the kinks out that the long hours at the computer had caused. Before she could step out of the cubicle, however, her partner suddenly appeared, and hurried her back inside.

"You've got to see this," Ryan said, sitting down at his own desk opposite Dominique's. "Pull up a chair."

Dominique pushed her squeaky desk chair around beside Ryan's. He had his laptop loading something, and a grim, but satisfied look on his face. "I think we may have found something to help Mr. Morris, Dom."

She felt a sudden uprising of emotion. Ryan barely knew the Morrises, and had, in the past, shown some mild resentment of Wally because of her sleuthing, yet he was just as invested in helping the family as the rest of their friends. That, coupled with Chief Jaeger's defense of Dominique and Ryan staying on the investigation, was almost enough to shake her composure. "What?"

"This is the recording of the GrovePAC performing arts center board of directors meeting a few months ago. Watch it and tell me what you think."

Dominique watched as the board members came into the room, greeting one another before taking their seats. Ryan fast forwarded through a section of people just sitting around, some looking at their watches, before Norman Fisch stood, clearly unwilling to wait any longer.

"I see in our packets that we are listing the theater as one that cannot accommodate live music during a theater production. The source of this information seems to be Wade Fuller." He paused, looking at each member of the committee. "He's saying we can only have canned music? Is he insane?"

Fisch had everyone's attention, not surprisingly, Dominique thought, due to his uncharacteristic outburst. The pharmacist was usually one of the most mellow people she knew. Without waiting for a response, Fisch made his point, "We didn't go to all the trouble to build a state of the art theater in order to only be able to have inferior entertainment."

The orchestra pit had been a big selling point to the

bondholders, Dominique knew. She and her husband had purchased some bonds as well as made donations. Supporting the arts had always been a priority in her family, and her husband's healthy dental practice allowed them the freedom to donate to several worthy causes.

But one of the selling features of the new space had been the ability to have staged musicals with live musicians. A feasibility study had determined that was a priority of the investors and potential audience.

"Wade said--" Henry Tolliver started, but he never had a chance to finish his thought.

"Who put Wade Fuller in charge of unilateral decisions?" Fisch demanded. "Granted, he is the chairman, but this is a committee, isn't it? Shouldn't the committee as a whole decide?"

"But he said it was just for now. He said—"

"Where is he?" Nate Morris asked. "Shouldn't he be here explaining, at the very least, his reasons for making it so that we can only have second rate musical productions?"

Fisch had taken a seat while Nate was talking and now he leaned forward, as if anxious to hear the answer to Nate's question.

"He had a big party coming into his restaurant," Tolliver explained.

Fisch looked at the man. "We all have businesses that require our attention."

"It will cost far more in the long run," Nate pointed out. "We can take a vote, which is how this should have been handled in the first place, and see where we are."

Fisch nodded his agreement.

The four other people in the room hadn't said a word. Of all of them, only one had sat on a town committee before, Dominique realized. She could see how it might be intimidating. But that didn't mean they should just knuckle under to whatever the chair said.

"All in favor of scrapping the orchestra pit say aye,"

said Beth Keegen. As secretary, she was charged with recording the vote. In the absence of the chairman, she could call the role.

When only one voice, Tolliver's, said "aye," Beth asked for the votes of those opposed, to be legal about the whole thing, as she explained. Five nays were heard. "The motion to defer building the pit, etc., has been defeated."

"You realize this could affect the magic show," Tolliver warned. "We gave the magician the dimensions for the stage and the location of the trap door without the addition of the pit. It is the premiere of our new theater and it is essential that the show go smoothly. Plus, now that you want to go ahead with building the pit, we'll never be ready in time."

Oscar Martinez, who had remained silent during the entire exchange, took off his reading glasses and put them on the table. He looked squarely at Tolliver. "I don't think you understand the nature of the pit. It involves a portable addition to the stage that can be reconfigured several ways, one of which is to enclose an orchestra. It is simple carpentry. Did you think it involved excavation? At this late date?" He picked up his glasses by the earpiece and held them, poised. "And how could any of that affect the location of the trap door and the use of the magician's lift?"

Tolliver looked as if he'd been played, which he obviously had. He had bought what Wade Fuller was selling without asking the right questions. Then again, Dominique thought, Tolliver was a yes man. They didn't ask questions.

Fisch's chair scraped on the wood floor of the room as he got on his feet again. "Before we all leave, I wanted to raise an issue that ordinarily would not be related to the business of this committee. As some of you know, there was a flood in the theater church, and an amateur production that was scheduled there became homeless. Other venues were sought but none proved viable as an alternate space. I am here today asking that we consider whether our new theater, which at the date of the show will still be officially unopened, could be used to do just one evening's performance."

No one spoke. Tolliver excused himself for a moment and rushed out.

Nate asked Fisch what would be involved as far as GrovePAC was concerned.

"To tell you the truth," Fisch said, "I have no idea. It was just something I thought I'd ask about. I could call in the director, and we could hear what he has to say." He shook his head. "It's just a crazy, desperate idea I had. I wasn't really expecting an answer right away."

"Go ahead and call the director," Beth Keegan said. Nate looked over at her. It looked to Dominique as if she winked back.

Fisch stood up. "Thank you. I'll e-mail you to set up the meeting."

As the meeting broke up Dominique leaned back in her chair and rubbed her eyes. Staring at the computer screen was getting to her. She was about to speak when Ryan held up his hand.

"Wait. There's more."

Dominique focused her eyes back on Ryan's laptop. A commotion outside the meeting room caused everyone to stop where they were. Wade Fuller swept into the room. He seemed to emanate bad vibrations.

It was clear that Henry Tolliver had called Fuller. And it was equally clear that he was angry.

"Who do you think you are, challenging me?" he thundered at Norman Fisch.

Fisch appeared stunned for a moment. But he recovered, and asked just exactly what Wade meant by that.

"I mean I was at my restaurant dealing with the evening rush, trying to make a living, and you people were here stabbing me in the back."

125

Fisch leaned back in his swivel chair and made a show of pondering that statement. Moving forward, he leaned on his elbow with his face cupped in the palm of his hand and a completely neutral expression on his face. After a long moment, during which Fuller fairly shook with rage, Fisch said, "Are you talking about the committee's decision to build the PAC to the original specifications that our supporters and trustees have agreed upon?"

Fuller started to open his mouth but Nate Morris stopped him. "The committee is not one man," he said. "Modifications are decisions to be made by all the members, not you alone. If you want to resign in protest, we will reluctantly accept your resignation."

"They should have been so lucky," Dominique muttered.

"Just what I was thinking," said Ryan. "But it gets better."

Put on a spot, Fuller capitulated. "Fine, fine. I'll go along on this. I really didn't want to make that other decision at all, and certainly not by myself, but you people don't make it easy to call emergency meetings."

He received a round of protests at that statement. "You are the only one available to meet during the day," Beth Keegan said, "yet you called all the meetings for early afternoon. Maybe we should call a vote and decide to put them back into the evening, when it is more convenient for the majority."

The opening and closing of Fuller's mouth reminded Dominique of a fish. "You all know why I asked that the meetings be early. My restaurant requires my attention at night."

"Nate's offer still stands," Fisch said. "If you can't fulfill the duties of chair, someone else will fill in for you."

Fuller seemed to consider it. But when he spoke it was only to offer to hold a few meetings at night, as they got closer to opening day and needed to handle last minute details.

"What about that other issue?" asked Tolliver. He apparently hadn't missed a thing during his phone call to Wade.

"There is no other issue," Wade said, his anger becoming visible again. "No way will we allow that amateur production. We are not going to sully our brand new theater with the likes of those people."

"What people, exactly?" Nate asked.

"You know who I mean. An amateur production here would set the wrong tone. We'd never be considered a bona fide PAC if we let in every little Girl Scout production."

Fisch looked amused for a moment, Dominique thought, as if contemplating his wife, Louise, as a Girl Scout, but then his annoyance took over. "We have agreed to look into it. You were not here for the vote."

"Let's vote again."

Keegan shook her head. "It wasn't even close. Let's not get ahead of ourselves, Wade."

He pounded his fist on the conference table. "This isn't over," he growled. Then he left the view of the camera. "You'll all be sorry."

Norman Fisch scratched his head. "Maybe he should have tried out for a part in the play. He's very dramatic."

The other members of the board didn't seem to share his enthusiasm.

Ryan turned off the sound and looked at Dominique. "That's the end of it. The rest is just conversation and them leaving. Do you think we may have something to go with here?"

"I do. Between this and the footage of Lance Palmer, there may be several more suspects to investigate. Great job. You may have saved our friend."

＃

After an unusually quiet dinner during which the

tension was thicker than the beef stew Wally had made with the first apple cider of the season, she went into her den and closed the door. Nate and Debbie were talking in the kitchen and, even though they were no longer talking about the case, Wally wanted to be elsewhere. She felt very tense because Debbie had not gone home with Elliot and she wanted to tell her that she should not be letting the case come between her and her husband, but she knew better than to open her mouth. Debbie thought she meddled in other people's lives, Wally knew, and she kept quiet about it, but she would not tolerate Wally saying anything about her own life.

Wally thought it was better to be in a quiet room, alone, so that she could think without anyone glaring at her, as Debbie had, or looking hurt, as Nate had, for thinking she didn't trust him. Elliot had given her a good idea, passed on from Dominique, something she should have thought up herself, and she was determined to implement it. A task to do, even if it was small and might not lead to anything, was better than nothing at all. Dominique's suggestion made her feel better and was, in a way, a vote of confidence. There were people on their side, Wally knew, and for that she was grateful.

She began by writing down the name of every person she could think of who might have had anything to do with Wade Fuller. She listed all the members of the GrovePAC committee, then added the names of the people involved in the play. "None of them would want to kill Wade, at least not in the theater on the night of the performance," she said to herself, hoping that Nate and Debbie were really out of earshot and would not come in and stop her from helping. "It would mean the end of the play."

But she listed them anyway. She wrote:

Lance Palmer-Argued with Wade Fuller on several occasions.

Babbette Fay-Left the chair below the stage and failed

to return on time.

Courtney Haven-?

She, along with the rest of the actors and crew, had not had any specific dealings with Wade that Wally knew about. She realized she had no idea about any of them or their potential relationships with Wade. The only person she could be sure about was Louise, and that was because she had an alibi.

It might be necessary to talk to them, individually, to see if they knew something that could help. She didn't look forward to talking to Courtney Haven.

Taking a fresh sheet of paper, she listed the people around town whom she heard had dealings with Wade.

Fergie- Wade had bad mouthed her to customers, costing her business

Telly-Wade had practically stolen the coveted liquor license from right under his big mustache.

Employees of Ristorante Marcella-Wade had a habit of yelling at his workers.

Former owner of Neon-Wade had stolen his last-chance chef.

Former chef-Rocco Something-Wade had fired him so her could hire Neon's chef. Wally would have to find out what his full name was and how to reach him.

Wally thought about the people she had just added to the list. Fergie, the florist, had also been involved with Wade. And their relationship had ended badly. Considering that, Wally contemplated listing Martha, poor Fergie's aunt, but that was impossible on so many levels, not least of which was she could still barely walk after the accident. Belle, Fergie's mother, was effectively a prisoner in her home without her sister or daughter to drive her around. She also seemed pretty weak, and no match for Louise who was probably heavier and would have been hard to drag into the storage closet, even with the smooth basement floors. Belle certainly could never have overpowered a man, even one such as Wade.

Telly, the owner of the restaurant that Wally and Nate frequented, came to mind as a suspect, since Wade had aced him out of the liquor license he'd been bidding for. "But that was nothing compared to what the owner of Neon might have felt," Wally muttered. The restaurant had closed because Wade lured the chef away. He could have been sufficiently frustrated to want to kill Wade, especially after all the expensive renovations had put him even further in the hole, financially. He'd spent at least as much on the Neon renovations as Wade Fuller had spent on Marcella's, yet he'd lost all his business along with his chef right after the reopening.

"I have to go see him," Wally said.

This talking-to-herself thing was making her self-conscious, even though she was alone. She wished there was someone she could talk to about this, but there wasn't. She had to proceed alone.

The people in his own restaurant might have had issues with Wade, Wally thought. He had been a hard driving person, and had not endeared himself to anyone she could think of. In fact, now that she was thinking of it, had someone been trying to run him down the day Martha was nearly struck by the van? Maybe that could lead somewhere. She picked up the desk phone and punched in the number.

Dominique answered on the first ring and Wally immediately tried to put her at ease. "I am not calling about Nate," she said.

"Okay," Dominique said, warily.

"I promise."

"Good. How are you doing?"

"About as well as can be expected. And I am doing what you said. I just had a question."

"I'll answer it if I can."

"Okay. Have you made any progress on who almost

ran down Martha Knight and her sister?"

"It isn't a high priority case," Dominique told her. "Why do you ask?"

"Because it occurred to me that perhaps it wasn't an accident and the hit-and-run driver was aiming for someone else."

"The only other person there was Wade Full—oh, I see where you are headed with this. I'll tell you what. I'll have a look at that file and if there is anything useful in it, I'll follow up."

Wally felt a tiny bit of hope. At least something was being done, related to Wade but not connected to Nate. "Thanks. I don't suppose I could get a look at it?"

"Sorry," said Dominique, "but I'll give you whatever I can. Let's hope you're onto something."

When Wally hung up she felt renewed energy. Good. She had to plan for how she was going to get to talk to all those people. And she was going to keep her ears open in case there were any more suspects.

But there was one thing she could not do to get a sense of people's feelings for Wade. She could not go to his funeral. Not with Nate under suspicion. She knew someone who could, however, someone who also had her finger on the pulse of Grosvenor. She knew just the right person for the job.

Wally's next call was to Louise.

"Whatever I can do," said Louise. "I know Nate didn't do it."

"That's a good start, but we need to find out who did. Nothing less will get him off the hook."

"Aren't the police the ones to do that?"

"They're taking too long," said Wally. "We can't live with this hanging over our heads."

"Hmm. I see your point. So how can I help?"

"I want to talk to everyone who was in the cast. I'm also going to talk to the crew members." Wally knew just who she wanted to talk to first, Babbette, the person in charge of costumes and sets.

"That's a lot of people," said Louise.

"Exactly. That's where you come in. If we split the job, it'll take less time. Plus, I might be kind of off-putting to a few of them, considering Nate's predicament."

"When should I start?"

"As soon as possible. Start with the younger ones first. I don't think they'll take much time, since I'm sure none of them would have wanted to do anything that would stop the show, and that's exactly what killing Wade did."

"I can't just ask them if they know who killed Wade, can I?"

"No," Wally said. "But you can ask them if they saw anything while they were rehearsing or earlier that day, or if they know anyone who might have held a grudge against Wade, or if they heard anyone talking about him."

"Okay," said Louise. "I'll see what I can do."

"One more thing. Could you please go to the funeral and see what you can find out?"

"I wouldn't miss it."

Wally let out the breath she had been holding. "Thanks."

#

Wally didn't waste any time. The next afternoon, as soon as school was out, she met with Babbette Fay in the Grove diner. After ordering lunch, Wally got right to the point. "I know you told the police that you weren't able to get back to the theater in time to send the chair back up and that you had to call Louise to ask her to do it."

"That's right," said Babbette. She seemed defensive. It didn't change anything, since Wally needed answers, but she thought she might want to pull back a bit. This was so important, but coming on too strong was not going to help.

"What happened to Louise might have happened to you, if you were the one in the basement," Wally said.

132

"And it certainly wasn't your fault that Louise was." Babbette wasn't looking especially guilty as she sat sipping her diet cola, Wally noted.

But the statement had the effect of giving her something to think about, which was exactly what Wally wanted her to do. "I still can't understand how someone even knew that the lift was down there," said the set designer. "If it hadn't been, or if the chair wasn't on it, there would not have been a place for the murderer to kill Wade."

"Whoever killed him would probably have found another place to leave him to bleed to death," Wally said.

"Why was Wade even down there?" Babbette asked. "I can't figure it out. He was planning on staying away from the theater while the 'stupid amateur play' was on, his words, not mine, and he wasn't going to come back until it was over, so he could assess the damage."

Wally felt as if her body would jump out of her seat. "How do you know that?"

"Because that's what he told me. And he didn't say it nicely. It was that way every time I saw him, even if I just passed him on the street, which I did that afternoon, in the parking lot."

"What did he say?"

"I'll be there right after the performance to make sure you didn't damage anything." She waited while the waitress brought their lunches. After putting ketchup on her plate, she added, "I told him if he was so worried, he should come watch the show." She popped a fry into her mouth, chewed, swallowed and laughed. "I was so afraid that the house would be empty that I was going around telling everyone to come see the show, even him. As it turned out, we were sold out."

"So what did he say to that?"

"He looked at me and said he'd had a busy day and was going to work until the show was over, that he didn't have time to waste, and that his restaurant staff needed to see his face more than I did."

Wally put down her salad fork. "What does that mean?"

Babbette shook her head. "I don't know and I didn't care."

"What time was that?"

"Around three, when I was dropping my daughter off at her ballet class."

"What was he doing there?"

Waving a French fry, Babbette said, "Oh, he wasn't right there. He was just getting out of his car at the restaurant. It's across the street from the ballet school. I had parked near his restaurant because there were no spaces across the street."

Wally thought about that. Something didn't sound right. "He wasn't at the restaurant for the lunch crowd?"

"Beats me," said Babbette, before taking a big bite of her hamburger.

Wally tried one or two other questions on Babbette but she didn't seem to have any more information, other than she hadn't seen Wade inside the theater at all that day and hadn't particularly noticed anyone talking to him during the course of the rehearsals. She changed the subject and asked about Babbette's daughter. Wally only half listened, though, and looked forward to lunch ending. It was time to move on to the next person on her list.

Chapter Fifteen

"I'm not hungry," said Wally. "But thanks."

Under Telly's mustache, he frowned. "It's tonight's special. I could use your opinion."

Wally found herself caving in. She'd had a virtuous lunch just hours earlier, after all, not even taking a single French fry when Babbette had offered. But all that willpower was going out the window at the thought of getting a preview of one of Telly's creations. From where she sat at one of the smaller side tables in his restaurant, she could smell divine odors emanating from the kitchen.

"Maybe just a bite," she said, promising herself to eat a small dinner.

Telly's face lit up. "I'll be right back."

While he was gone Wally reflected on his demeanor. She didn't really believe that he could have been the one to kill Wade and still be his usual cheerful self a few days later while Nate was under suspicion, but she was here to get answers and they might not all be verbal. It paid to watch body language.

When he returned with a small plate featuring a mushroom and goat cheese tart, Wally sighed. Not only was it way more than a "bite," it smelled delicious. She knew that plate would be empty when she was finished. Maybe skipping dinner would be a good idea. Nate would have to eat, though. Which brought her back from the little bit of heaven in her mouth to the problems at hand.

"It's delicious," she told Telly. "My compliments to the chef."

He beamed. "Thank you, Madame. It did turn out well. It could become a regular item, if people like it as much as you do."

"I'll look forward to that," Wally said. "And I'll tell Nate to order it next time we come."

"Which will be soon, I hope."

Wally shrugged. "Things are kind of difficult right now."

Telly's face clouded. "I do not believe your husband is a murderer."

"Thanks, but we have to make sure the police believe in his innocence too."

"Is there something I can do?"

Wally looked at him. He seemed eager, hopeful, not at all nervous. But suddenly he was tense, looking over her shoulder.

"Is something wrong?"

Telly sighed. "It's Rolly. He's out in the middle of the road again."

Wally turned to look out the window at the man in tattered sweats. He was indeed standing on the yellow line in the middle of Grove Avenue. "Isn't it kind of early in the day?" she asked Telly, after he'd called 9-1-1.

"He's getting worse," Telly answered, although he kept his eyes on Rolly. "This is the third time today he's been out there. And he's started drinking more heavily, which I was told is bad with his meds. I'm afraid they are going to take him away this time. He's a danger to himself and others."

"Maybe it's for the best," said a voice. Wally turned and saw one of the waitresses also looking out the window. She was watching another waitress, Stacey, the one who had helped Rolly out of the road on the night Wally first saw him standing out there. Stacey again went into the street and helped Rolly onto the curb. She stayed with him until the police arrived a few seconds later.

Telly went to the door and called out to Stacey. "If you want to ride down there with him, go ahead. We'll be okay."

He turned back to Wally. "The lunch rush is over," he told her, by way of explanation, "and there are hours until dinner, with the exception of the early birds."

"Stacey seems to be as soft-hearted as her boss," said Wally. "I've seen her help Rolly before."

"I think they went to school together," Telly said. He began taking Wally's empty plate away. "Coffee? We can have it together and then you can ask me whatever you want."

As he went into the kitchen Wally felt heat rise to her face. She hadn't realized just how transparent she was. But then another thought occurred to her. Could Telly be putting on an act since he knew she was there to question him? Pushing the thought away, Wally opted to believe the best—just as long as it didn't impede Nate's defense.

When Telly returned he brought out two espressos and a small plate of chocolate hazelnut truffles. Wally resolved to skip breakfast too.

"Telly," she said, after sipping her coffee, "I need your help. Someone was angry enough to kill Wade Fuller. You are in the same business. Is there anything you can tell me about anyone who might have hated him that much?"

"Oh, I could name a few people who hated Wade's guts." Telly stroked his mustache. "There were several people bidding on that liquor license that Wade bought."

"Did he bid that much more than everyone else?"

"He wasn't even in the running, not at first. Then suddenly he came up with $250,000. He won hands down."

That number was far too familiar to Wally. But she didn't understand the timing. Wade didn't have that money until the day of his murder. Or did he? Did Fred Neimeyer actually get it to him before Nate lent him the money? It was worth looking into.

"What I don't understand," said Telly, "is how he had so much money after renovating the restaurant? And where did he get it? Last year at this time he was talking about having to close down the restaurant."

"Didn't he get a new chef? I heard he's wonderful. Not as good as yours," Wally hastily added.

"Of course not," Telly said, with a smile. His mustache never moved. "But he is good. He would have helped Neon be something other than an empty hulk of a restaurant."

"I heard the owner had to declare bankruptcy," said Wally. "Is that true?"

"Absolutely."

"Do you know where he is now?"

Telly shook his head. "Not a clue."

Wally made a mental note to follow up with Dominique. "I'm sorry you didn't get your liquor license."

"It's okay. It's not like I had it and lost it. Besides, I can still sell New Jersey wine, and I don't mind opening bottles that people bring in. If someone doesn't want to come to my restaurant and eat my fine food just because I can't serve hard liquor, so be it."

"I never understood why New Jersey wine was exempted from the liquor license requirement," said Wally. But she had more pressing questions. "Anyone else?"

"Oh, you know, the usual people. Anyone he's ever fired, and that would include the former chef. That was a bit sticky, if I recall. He had no clue he was about to be replaced, and did not even have a current resume."

"Do you know where the former chef is now?"

"Nope. For all I know, he and Barney, Neon's owner, could be planning to open a restaurant."

Another mental note went onto Wally's cerebral checklist. She worried, though, that she might forget something, so she stopped trying to be casual about her conversation with Telly and started making actual notes on a paper napkin. "What about the other business owners in town?"

"You can ask Nate about that, I'm sure. Wade made himself the center of every Chamber of Commerce meeting, and of course there was the whole GrovePAC thing. I read in the local paper how this was his project, like no one else had anything to do with it, and how he was going to protect the performing arts center while he charitably let the amateur performers use the theater."

Wally had been too busy to read the paper that week. She would have to dig a copy out of the recycling bin where the ever-efficient Nate would have already placed it, and see what had been said about Wade's claims. If Wade's proprietary attitude toward the theater had been published, it might be reasonable to believe whoever killed him was aware of it. Maybe that was how he was lured to the theater he had told Babbette he was avoiding. It was worth looking into.

"One more question," Wally said, wishing there was at least one more drop of espresso in her cup. As much as she liked espresso, there was just not enough to satisfy her craving for large cups of coffee.

"Ask me anything. I'm an open book."

Wally hoped so. "Someone told me that when she saw Wade outside his restaurant the afternoon he died, he had said he was just arriving for the day." That might not have been exactly what Babbette said, Wally knew, but it was close enough. "I thought that was odd."

"He was probably coming back from the association meeting."

"The restaurant association?"

"Yes. It was that day, at noon."

That puzzled Wally. "Doesn't that pose a problem for the members?"

"It does for me. If they schedule it for a Monday, when we're closed, I can go. But that Monday was Labor Day, so it was put off 'til Friday. It's always the first week of the month, so that's what they do for months with Monday holidays. I stayed here serving my customers. Wade probably went—he's the next president." A shocked look passed over Telly's face. "I guess he isn't anymore." He shook his head. "As much as that guy was a thorn in my side, I wouldn't have wished that horrible death on him."

Wally thanked Telly for the goodies and the information and picked up her purse. Telly asked her to wait a moment and disappeared into the kitchen, leaving her wondering where she'd start on processing all this information.

"Tell Nate I'm pulling for him," Telly said a few minutes later, as he handed her a bag for Nate's dinner. He wouldn't accept payment, so Wally promised she and Nate would be back soon. On the whole, it was a win-win situation for her. She loved the restaurant. And the best part was, she had some leads. New suspects, especially when one's husband already was one, were a very good thing.

#

"Thanks, Dominique," Wally said as she hung up the phone. She closed her eyes for a moment and made a wish that the information she'd given the detective would lead to something.

"Did Dominique find something?" Nate asked as he walked into the kitchen. He looked so hopeful Wally hated to have to let him down.

"She's looking into a few things," Wally said. She was about to add more when she realized that wasn't going to be necessary. Nate was onto another subject.

He looked around, puzzled, based on his knit eyebrows. "What are we making for dinner?" he asked.

140

Wally realized it was past six o'clock. Her stomach was still so full, dinner hadn't even entered her mind. "Nothing," she told him.

"Are we going out? I really don't think I want to—"

"No, we're not going out."

"Okay, then. I'll cook by myself." He went to the refrigerator. "Let's see what we have in—"

"You aren't cooking, either," Wally interrupted.

Nate put on his concept of a sad person's face. "Hmmm. I'm going to be so hungry."

Wally had to laugh. "No, you are going to have a wonderful meal." She opened the refrigerator and took out what Telly had sent. After a few minutes in the microwave, Nate was happily eating his dinner.

Between bites, he asked Wally why she wasn't eating and how his meal had come about. She told him about her visit to Telly's restaurant. The happy mood suddenly changed.

"You shouldn't have done that," Nate said.

His reaction surprised her. "Why not?"

"He's going to think that we think he could have been involved. He's my friend. If he knew anything at all, he would have told the police."

"He doesn't think that at all. Why is just talking to him such a bad thing?"

"Because he had nothing to do with the murder and your asking questions is only going to bring unnecessary attention to him. He's lost enough already."

"I don't think he feels that way at all. He wants to help."

"He can't help," Nate said abruptly. "He doesn't know anything about what Wade Fuller was up to. I wish you'd stay out of it. I feel bad enough already."

Wally didn't like Nate's tone at all, but she could understand it. He might have felt guilty that his money was used to thwart Telly's planned bar.

141

Now it was up to her to make him understand that some good might have come out of the conversation. "Telly gave me some information. I passed it along to Dominique. She seemed happy to have it." She paused to let that sink in. "For the moment I'm out of it." She stood up. "Enjoy your dinner."

She didn't look back as she grabbed Sammy's leash and went to the back door. Sammy, who spent his waking hours watching Wally's every move, was at her heel before she reached the threshold.

It was a beautiful early September evening. In just a few days the Jewish New Year, Rosh Hashanah would be upon them.

Sammy pulled Wally along. The black Lab was strong, but he didn't tug hard enough to pull Wally over. She was too annoyed to really think about where they would walk so she just let Sammy take her where he wanted. It was the most familiar route that Nate and Sammy walked, down toward the university. Wally wasn't about to walk that far, though, so she turned toward Grove Avenue, which would make a big loop and lead back home.

The peacefulness of walking with Sammy, once he settled down and stopped pulling so hard, began to relax Wally. It gave her time to appreciate her surroundings and the benefits of the season. Peeled bark from London Plane trees crunched under her feet and cascades of dry leaves swirled down to the street whenever there was a little gust of wind. It wasn't autumn yet, but it was on its way.

A familiar figure was ahead of her on the street. Rolly. It was hard to believe he was already back on the street after his dangerous walk through traffic. Maybe Stacey, the waitress, had talked the police out of keeping him in custody. She was obviously fond of Rolly. Wally wondered if the feelings were reciprocated.

Rolly didn't seem to be getting into any trouble, which was a relief to Wally, considering how he had looked

142

earlier. That didn't keep her from worrying about the young man and wishing there was a way she could help him. He was always around town, looking a little lost, even more so lately.

"How are you Rolly?" Wally asked.

He seemed a bit puzzled. "Okay, Mrs. um…"

Wally realized that Rolly was having trouble recognizing her. "I'm Wally."

"Oh, yes."

"How are you? Are you feeling okay?"

Rolly looked at the ground. "That's a nice dog," he said.

Wally let the subject of Rolly's health go. "Thanks. His name is Sammy and he's very friendly. You can pet him if you'd like."

The look on Rolly's face as he stroked Sammy could have been a testimonial to the healing and calming power of dogs. When Rolly stood up a few moments later, he looked like a changed man. Wally hoped it would last.

When Rolly had moved on, she continued her walk. Her route led right past Wade's restaurant, which was clearly closed. The murder had happened only a few days earlier, so that was no surprise, but it made Wally wonder if it would ever open again.

She looked at it closely, wondering if it held any secrets or clues to who murdered the owner. The employees had all been questioned, according to Dominique, but had not had any helpful information. Yet Wally was convinced there were people who knew something relevant but just didn't realize it. At lunch Babbette had given her information that Dominique and the other detectives didn't have, but only because Wally had chatted her up. It was possible that with enough conversation, some other clues might emerge.

Wally looked across the street. The ballet school, where Babbette was taking her daughter the day that Wade

143

accosted her, was a small house that had been converted into a studio. It was right next to Blossoms, the florist's shop owned by Fergie Schultz. Seeing it made Wally stop to think. Had someone really been trying to run down Wade the day Fergie's mother and aunt had come to visit her?

The sound of a car horn snapped Wally out of her reverie. As she turned she could feel Sammy's tail wagging wildly before she even saw Elliot at the curb, with his window down. "How are you Sammy?" Elliot said. "And you, Wally?"

"We're both fine. What are you doing here?" Wally took a close look at her son-in-law, hoping to see whether the strain that had been on his face the last time she saw him had disappeared. It had not.

"I'm wracking my brain, to tell the truth," Elliot said. "I'm trying to think of a way to help, so Nate can be cleared and things between Debbie and me will get back to normal." He frowned. "She's a bit touchy right now."

Elliot was lucky he'd missed Debbie's teen years, Wally mused. "I'm sorry to hear that. She'll be fine, once this is all over. We all will." That last bit was more to herself, as she thought about why she was out there with Sammy at this hour.

"Why don't you and Sammy hop in? I'll take you home."

"Want to go for a ride in the car?" Wally asked the dog. He did, as evidenced by his squeezing his body into the car the moment she opened the door. "Go into the back," she directed him. "I get the front."

"Don't drive just yet," Wally said to Elliot once she was seated. "We should talk. Are you keeping up with the case?"

"Yes, of course."

"Is there anything you can tell me?"

"I talked to Dominique," Elliot said. "She told me

144

about your phone call."

"I'm hoping it will lead to something." Wally turned toward the restaurant. "All those people out of work."

"They won't be for long. I understand the restaurant will be opening next week, right after the memorial service."

"Who will run it?"

"Mrs. Fuller. She supposedly told her friends that it was her husband's dream and she would keep it alive for him."

That was contrary to what Wally would have expected. She had thought the woman resented all the time Wade spent in the restaurant. Then again, it was what kept her in manicures and designer clothes. But if she'd wanted to be in the business, why would she wait until her husband was dead to mention it? Or was she doing it out of a feeling of obligation? Or, had Wade kept her out of the restaurant when she really wanted to be part of it?

"I see you have some questions. There is nothing there. Dominique checked. Mrs. Fuller hadn't seen her husband at all that day, although she did speak to him on the phone. She was away that morning and only got home a half hour before the performance started."

Wally was grateful for the information, but sorry there were no leads. "So is there anything you can do?"

"I wish there was. I'm not on the case at all, and assistant prosecutor Dane will make sure I get into trouble if I interfere. But I keep hoping there's at least something I can do."

"Me too. I was so sure when I went to talk to each of them that Telly and Babbette would have some important information."

"They didn't?"

"Well, not exactly. But I did get an explanation about something Babbette said, and it came from Telly."

"What was that?"

"I found out that Wade probably went to a restaurant association meeting on the day he was killed."

"He did?"

"Don't the police know that? It was a regular meeting. It must have been on his appointment calendar."

Elliot shook his head. "It wasn't. Or actually, they didn't find an appointment calendar."

"Nothing?"

"Not yet, anyway. So I guess that's why no one has mentioned the meeting. We should get Dominique right on that."

Wally felt awful. "I should have mentioned it to her when I called."

"Don't worry about it. I'll take care of it. Maybe it'll score me some points with Debbie." He looked in the rear-view mirror. "Sammy, have you finished sniffing the car? You won't find any crumbs, Saffron already checked."

"How is the puppy?" Wally asked.

"She's fine. But Debbie keeps looking at her as if she was a traitor."

"The tooth marks on the sunglasses?"

"The police might not have been able to prove they were Nate's otherwise."

"Yes they would," Wally said. "They were prescription. Saffron isn't to blame, for that, anyway."

Elliot started the car. "It's time to face the music."

Chapter Sixteen

Nate was waiting on the front porch when they drove up. He stood stiffly while Wally got out of the car and let Sammy out behind her. Elliot gave a wave and drove off.

"Come inside please," Nate said. His tone was measured and glum. But as soon as they were inside he took Wally into his arms and hugged her. "I'm so sorry about before. I know you were only trying to help when you went to see Telly. Please forgive me."

Wally stepped back and looked up at him. "Nate, you know almost everyone in town. They're all your friends. But one of them may have killed Wade. I might have to step on some toes in order to clear you, but that is exactly what I'm going to do. "

Then she went back into his arms and held onto him as tightly as she could. She wished she could stay there forever, or at least until their problems went away. But they didn't seem as if they would be going away on their own and it was up to Wally, and Nate too, to take care of them.

"Louise called," Nate said over Wally's shoulder.

Wally was out of the embrace like a shot. "What did she say?"

"She wouldn't say anything. I've never heard her not say anything for an entire conversation. I got the sense there was something going on between you two. Is there anything I should know?"

"I don't know. Let me call and see what she found out."

"About . . . ?"

"What do you think? She's going around asking members of the cast if they know anything." Wally had a momentary spasm of worry. "I'm only hoping she does it with finesse."

Nate's blue-green-eyed stare only increased her nervousness. She shook it off and dialed her friend.

Louise sounded positively cheery when she answered the phone. "I talked to almost everyone. That Lance is so nice."

"Did he have anything to say about the murder?"

"Hoooh, boy did he. He blamed theater ghosts. I asked him how that was possible and he just said it was obvious. Ever since Maggie Mattoon whistled, things have gone wrong. The plumbing, the flood, and so on. And he thinks it may have cost him his career."

"Oh, I'm sorry to hear that. What else did you find out?"

"Well," Louise said, sounding as if she were launching into a major gossip fest, "the Clark's are squabbling and he moved out. Courtney got a bit part in Law and Order, so she's thrilled, and now is actually nice to me, and Doug Norton is thinking of moving to Florida to be near his daughter."

Wally felt a new sensation, frustration. "That's nice, but did any of them tell you anything about what they saw that night?"

"No. None of them was on stage when it happened. They weren't in the back hall either, except for Courtney, but that wasn't until right before she was supposed to go on."

"Come on," said Wally, regretting that her frustration was making her question her friend. "No one at all is a smoker? The alley would be the only place to go smoke, and the only way back there from inside the theater would be from the back hall."

"What alley?"

"The one where Wade made Babbette and me paint the furniture and props. It's right behind the theater, although you can't see it from the street. You have to go down a driveway to the left of all the stores. It runs the whole length behind them, for deliveries and things."

"No one said anything about going out to smoke."

Wally had to let that go. The police would have asked that anyway. "What about the stage crew kids?"

"I haven't reached any of them. They are all in school. I left messages."

"Thanks," said Wally. "Maybe one of them saw something."

"What's next?" Louise asked.

"I think someone needs to talk to Wade's wife. And his step-daughter."

Louise gasped. "Would that someone be me?"

"Do you think you could do it?"

"Wouldn't you rather do it yourself?"

"Yes, I would," Wally said, "but do you really think she'd talk to me while people think my husband killed her husband?"

"Uh, I guess not. But I have no guarantee she'll talk to me either."

Wally agreed but didn't mention that.

"She might think I'm trying to get her to let me sell her house," Louise said, "since now that Wade is gone, it might seem a bit big for her. That would be awful."

"You'd never be so predatory."

"Right. Okay, I'll do the best I can," Louise promised. "And while I'm doing that, what will you be doing?"

"I'm going to talk to some people who weren't on your list."

After she hung up Wally filled in Nate on Louise's

149

efforts. He shrugged. "I'm sure you two aren't going to get anything out of anyone that the police didn't get."

"Don't be such a naysay—" she broke off as a thought hit her. "That's who we need to talk to, and I guarantee the police don't have a clue about her."

"Her? Who?"

"Mrs. Naysayer. Wanda Neimeyer. She might know something—at the very least about her brother's blackmailing of Fred. It was his fault, or at least it was because of his problems, that you are in this to begin with."

Nate looked at her in disbelief. "Are you forgetting about my sunglasses, hat, and utility knife being found near the area of the murder?"

"No, I'm not. But they would have been more likely to believe you if the exact same amount of money that was going in and out of Wade's account weren't inexplicably going in and out of yours."

"I don't know about that, but I do know that Wanda is not going to want to talk to either of us about what was going on. Why would she tell us whether she wanted the money for herself or Wade, and--"

"I think it's fairly likely she wanted it for Wade," Wally cut in, "after all, that's who Fred's money, er, our money, went to in the end." Wally knew she sounded sour, but it was getting hard to keep her temper under control.

"Okay," said Nate, "let's say she was being altruistic toward her brother by blackmailing her husband of however many years. Then what? Do you think she then went out and killed Wade?"

"No, of course not. But she might know more about his business than we do."

"We know nothing about his business."

"So you admit I'm right?"

"Pardon me?"

"Wanda would be a good person to question," Wally explained. "But we can't do it and we can't ask anyone to do it or they will wonder why we are interested in what she has to say."

"But she's Wade's sister. Wouldn't that be enough reason?"

"Good point. I'll suggest it to Dominique."

Nate sighed. "Please do it carefully. We worked so hard to protect Fred, I don't want to accidentally blow it now."

Wally shook her head in frustration. "Fine. Just one thing, though. With all this protection we are doing for Fred, are you sure he didn't kill Wade? He had good reasons, well, reason, anyway."

Nate looked at Wally. "I don't think he could have done that, but I honestly don't know for sure."

#

The sirens awoke Wally at two a.m. She rolled over, hoping that no one was hurt.

Dominique's call awoke her again when it came at 6:15. "Can you come over later this morning?"

"To the station?"

"Huh?" Dominique seemed flustered. "No, I'm sorry, I'm only half awake. Come to the performing arts center."

"What happened?"

"There was a fire. The production manager, Harvey Floyd, was injured. They don't know if he's going to make it."

Wally's heart leaped in her chest. She could barely wrap her mind around the pain he must be in. "Oh, my--. Wait," she said, interrupting herself, "what happened to the sprinklers?"

"There weren't any in the closet where we found him."

Relief flooded over her. "So he wasn't burned?"

"No, it's smoke inhalation. But it's really serious."

"The closet—"

"Yes, Wally, it's the same one where Louise was found."

151

Not again. "Do you think he knew some--?"

"Just come over, please. When you wake up."

"I'm up."

There were still two fire engines outside GrovePAC when Wally arrived. Since the fire station was only a few blocks away, Wally supposed that those sirens she had heard were coming from other towns. How big had the fire been?

"I'm glad you're here," said Dominique when Wally, dressed for work even though it was hours away, joined her in the basement underneath the stage. The walls were all blackened and water pooled on the floor. "They are just about finished combing the place and they suspect an accelerant was used. I wanted to get your impression, since you were down here last week."

"Is there any more word on Harvey? He's a nice man. And he was helpful during the rehearsals, even though he didn't have to be. Tillie will be so upset."

Dominique shook her head, putting a stop to Wally's ramblings. "Not yet. But he's hanging in there."

That didn't reassure Wally much. "How did he get into the closet?"

"We don't know exactly, but there is evidence that he may have crawled in there and collapsed."

"Why would he do that?"

"Perhaps, to avoid the smoke, he got down on his hands and knees and he got lost in the dark. A fire, especially a smoky one like this one supposedly was, blots out everything, even emergency lighting."

Dominique's partner, Ryan, interrupted them to say that the fire captain was releasing the area. They could look around the basement at will but they were to stay out of the alley, because the fire was started just inside the door. That area was still under investigation.

"What was he doing here in the middle of the night?" Wally asked.

"We don't know. The theater is scheduled to open Saturday night. Maybe he was working on some last minute things."

Talk of the opening gave Wally a jolt. Her family, as well as Dominique and her husband, James, had tickets for the opening and the gala afterwards. Wally hadn't thought about it at all since they bought the tickets, she'd been so wrapped up in *"Anyone Else"* and its aftermath. This gave her another thought. "Does this get Nate off the hook for Wade's murder? He was home with me all night."

"We don't even know if the two are related," said Dominique. "And you know it isn't up to us. Ms. Dane and the rest of the prosecution team have to see it the way we do."

Wally could only hope. And while she was at it, say a prayer for Harvey Floyd.

#

"I cannot believe what you're telling me," Louise said when Wally showed up on her doorstep at seven-thirty. She'd called first to say she was coming and bringing muffins.

"Which part can't you believe?"

"Well, let's see. There's the fact that you bought muffins instead of making them, first of all." She held up her hand and ticked off one finger. "Then there is this whole thing about a fire possibly being set and Harvey Floyd being the intended victim." She ticked off another finger. Then her eyes got wide. "Did I say intended? He was the victim. Is he going to be okay?"

Wally shrugged. "I hope so. Maybe he can tell the police who else was in the theater. Maybe this whole thing will be over, finally."

"But what if he can't? What if it isn't related? What if he just caught someone breaking in and the person got the better of him?"

Wally didn't say anything. Those same thoughts had

run through her mind.

"I'm sorry," said Louise. "Of course this is going to send a signal to the powers that be that they are barking up the wrong tree."

"I hope so."

"What did Nate say when you told him about the fire?" Louise asked.

"First he said 'umph.'"

"Why?"

"He's not at his best when awakened from a sound sleep. Then, when I told him I was going to meet Dominique, and why, he wanted to go with me, but I didn't think the rest of the police force would tolerate him being there. So I went alone. He had an early meeting in Short Hills today, anyway."

"Lucky for me," said Louise, "or he'd be eating these muffins right now. More coffee?"

Wally put up her hand. "No, I'm practically swimming already. I had at least four cups while we were waiting for more reports."

"And?"

"And nothing. The police are still considering Nate the main suspect. And I am still investigating. I wanted to talk to Dominique about what you told me, but I didn't get a chance."

"Maybe she has time now," Louise said. "You should call her."

"I'll do it when I get home."

"It's going to work out," Louise said. "I'll call you after the funeral."

#

Wally called Dominique before she went to work. She only had a minute to talk, but Dominique gave what information she could about each of the people on Wally's list, which included everyone she could think of.

Dominique made special mention of Lance, and after

Wally prodded, admitted that she had seen video of an altercation between him and Wade two days before the murder. "I tried to see if that would lead anywhere," she explained to Wally, "but several people were with him every minute from the time he arrived at the theater until the murder was discovered. It was the same when we viewed the tapes of the members of the performing art center board. They all had reason to hate Wade Fuller, but there was no evidence pointing at any of them."

"Thanks for trying," Wally said. Then she mentioned the name she really cared about, as if it were an afterthought. She didn't want to raise any suspicions when she asked about Wanda Neimeyer, the sister of the deceased, but she had to know.

"Why do you ask?"

"I thought she might know something about her brother's business, something that maybe others wouldn't know."

"As a matter of fact," said Dominique, "we are all wondering why Mrs. Neimeyer's husband gave Mr. Fuller the money that was in his account. That same amount of money was only borrowed that afternoon but was paid back to Nate. Is there something you want to tell me?"

"Definitely not."

"Oh." Dominique sounded disappointed.

"I just wondered if Mrs. Neimeyer or her husband had anything to say about the murder."

"You know they are separated, right?"

That separation was the cause of everything, in Wally's opinion. "Yes."

"First of all, they were not in the same room when they were questioned. But they told exactly the same story about the money. It was a loan to Mr. Fuller, and when the expected financing for that loan didn't come through in time for him to purchase the liquor license, your husband picked up the slack."

Wally couldn't believe that Nate had willingly contributed to stealing the liquor license from under Telly's nose. Fred Neimeyer must not have mentioned what the money was for when he asked for Nate's help. No wonder he'd been so moody. "Do you think they told you everything?"

"I don't know. I don't even know if they know, but for two people who can't get along, they certainly made an effort to compare their stories."

That puzzled Wally, considering how vicious their breakup had been. Both had said horrible things about each other, quite publicly. But if it was all as Dominique said, maybe there was a reason. At the very least, both of them would want their names kept out of it. "Did either of them have any idea who would want to kill Wade?"

"Mr. Neimeyer seemed to have despised his brother-in-law," said Dominique. "The wife seemed truly sad, but not necessarily surprised. I got the feeling she knew her brother was not well liked."

"That's somewhat of an understatement," Wally said in a tone as equally sarcastic as Dominique's. "But I guess that's what happens when a person treats people so badly."

"Anyone in particular?"

Wally could think of a few and one specifically, but she made a sudden decision to confront that person herself. There were several things she wanted to ask.

"Not really. Thanks for your help. I'll let you get back to work."

#

After a morning of fun in the late summer sun, songs, and crafts with her preschool class, Wally went to see Fergie in Blossoms, her flower shop. She looked frazzled, but Wally supposed that was because it was getting to be a busy season, with the Jewish holidays approaching.

"How is your aunt?" Wally asked.

"Much better. I think she'll be out of rehab pretty

soon."

Wally didn't want to waste Fergie's time, though, so she told her to go ahead and keep filling her orders. The chance to see so many beautiful flowers was an added bonus.

Fergie selected a large glass vase from under her work bench and placed delphinium, pink roses, Shasta daisies, and some greens inside. When she added a last stargazer lily, another gorgeous Blossoms original arrangement was finished. She made it look so simple that Wally was envious. Her own attempts to arrange flowers look more like clumps of colors and shapes, and were far from beautiful.

"Did you see Wade the night of the play?" Wally asked, thinking of "play" as a euphemism for "murder." She didn't think it would help to mention it specifically.

"No," Fergie said. "I delivered the flowers much earlier in the day on the way to the synagogue deliveries. Silk flowers are no substitute for the real thing," she continued, her eyes on the next creation, "and I was doing them gratis, but they said they could not be real because of some superstition. That is, except for the ones for the actors afterward."

"Who put them into the vases?"

"I'm not sure. I was going to arrange them on the way back from my last delivery, but I got a rush order. They didn't need to be done until later, anyway. Since they weren't real they could be arranged at any time."

Somehow that hadn't happened, Wally thought, remembering back to how the vases had looked. They were hardly remarkable, except for their skimpiness, and each vase just had one type of flower. There was no "arrangement" about them.

Fergie frowned. "I had always planned to, but then I wasn't able to make it. I hope whoever did it made them look pretty." She looked up at Wally and gave a small

157

gasp. "Not that it mattered, in the end."

"If you don't mind my asking," said Wally, "what delayed you? It was an important night and a good opportunity to show off your beautiful arrangements."

Fergie turned disappointed eyes to Wally. "I know. The only consolation I have is that no one saw, once Wade's b--" She broke off.

Clearly, at least to Wally, Fergie still had feelings for him. "I'm sorry. I know this must be hard for you."

Fergie swept some leaves off her work table. "And I know why you are asking. The question is do you think I had something to do with Wade's murder?"

"I'm just trying to find people who might have seen something," Wally said, feeling her own emotions rise, but keeping her voice even, if not warm. "You were supposed to be there. That's why I'm here. But if you weren't at the theater, I guess you can't help me."

"I'm sorry," Fergie said, and she sounded as if she meant it. "I really can't help you."

\#

Wally stopped in at the bakery next to the entrance to the train station. It was a busy place, especially since the first night of Rosh Hashanah was approaching. People were placing and picking up their orders for seasonal baked goods for family dinners. Usually Wally had her family and Nate's mother to dinner and she included Louise and Norman and their children, but this year, with all that was going on, she was totally relinquishing her hosting role. Louise had invited Nate and Wally for dinner after the first day of services, and they would be going to Rachel's for the second evening.

The very thought of the upcoming series of High Holiday services, when the synagogue would actually be full, at least on the first day, gave Wally an uneasy feeling. No one had said anything about the suspicion surrounding Nate the previous Saturday when they attended Shabbat services, but that was the usual group, the ones who knew Nate. Anyone who knew Nate knew he was innocent, but what about those people who didn't know him? High Holiday services also drew people who seldom went to synagogue, many who had never met Nate.

Would someone mention the trouble? Would people look at him strangely when he emptied his pockets of his "sins" during the ritual casting out of sins held at the river near the duck pond? Were there people they knew who really believed Nate could have done such a thing? Until now that ritual had been a pleasurable experience for Wally. She taught her nursery school class about it by letting them throw Cheerios into water that, for the occasion, replaced the sand in the sand table. The children didn't fully understand it, but it helped explain the concepts of celebrating the New Year and going through the ten Days of Awe that led to Yom Kippur, the Day of Atonement. Children didn't fast, of course, but Wally explained that to them too.

It was a joyful and profound time of year. This year, though, Wally didn't feel ready to face it.

She shook herself. If she could find out who killed Wade, and maybe even who attacked Harvey Floyd, this nightmare would be over. It wasn't just an inconvenience, it was eating into Wally, and she knew it was also eating into Nate. There was a tension in him that he never had before, except when his father had been near the end. Wally felt sorry for her husband. It was so wrong for anyone to think he could have committed the crime.

She drove to Neon, the restaurant that had closed shortly after its chef went to work at Wade Fuller's restaurant, and parked in the lot behind it. When she got to the entrance she found a phone number on the door to call in case of emergencies. Wally pulled out her cell phone and dialed. Three rings later she had Barney Emmons, the owner of the restaurant, on the phone—in Florida. When he answered, she started walking back to her car.

"I heard Wade got whacked," Barney said.

Wally stopped walking and sucked in her lips. She had only met Barney on one occasion, and he hadn't struck her as the type of person to make light of a murder. Maybe he had been watching too much of the <u>Sopranos</u>. Maybe he had those kinds of connections—it wasn't unheard of in New Jersey to be involved in organized crime.

Deciding that was too unlikely, Wally continued to her car and proceeded with her planned questions, after murmuring some suitable response. "When did you decide to sell your liquor license to Wade?"

"After he stole my chef and put me out of business. Only I didn't decide to sell it to him. I was going to sell it to Telly White."

"How did Wade get it then?"

Barney sighed loudly. "By the time I closed the restaurant I was so far into debt that I had no choice but to take what I could get. Fuller was offering twice what Telly put up. It was a no brainer."

"But you had an agreement with Telly, right?"

"What am I, a charity? No, I couldn't settle for Telly's money."

"No one else was bidding?"

"No one else was even in the ballpark. I only wish Fuller would've taken the restaurant, too. He wouldn't have had to spend all that money on remodeling. My space was first class."

Even if Wally agreed with that assessment, she thought, as she opened her car and got inside, it wouldn't have made sense for Wade to relocate his restaurant to Barney's space. They were decorated in two completely different ways—Wade's was Tuscan, while Barney's was obviously supposed to be urban shabby chic.

"It was a shame about your restaurant," Wally said. "I heard you had to file for bankruptcy."

"I did," Barney admitted. "But now I have a clean slate. I can start over."

"Do you think you'll open another restaurant?"

"Could be, if I find the right chef. A chef can make or break a restaurant, you know."

"That's what happened to Neon, right?"

"If I'd only known that my chef was going to leave me, I'da never put all that money in. He knew it too, but off he went. I tried to double his salary, give him a share of the restaurant, anything. But he wouldn't stay."

"That must have been rough."

"It was awful. I felt like killing Fuller, if you really want to know. But let me avoid a misunderstanding--I didn't. I came down to Florida instead. A few days on the beach with a bottle of tequila and I was feeling no pain."

"Why didn't you try to get a new chef before you lost the restaurant?"

"Oh, I did. But word was out in the restaurant association about my space. It got a bad rep. So many failed ventures had gone into that space over the years. Too bad I didn't know about it before I bought in. And even after I heard what the history was, I was still sure I'd turn it around."

Wally could have told him about the history. It seemed the restaurant was having a grand opening with new management, name, and décor, every two years. It was a money pit. That it had a reputation in the association came as no surprise. "No chef would take a chance? Then how did you get the first one?"

"He came with me, from South Jersey. We'd been reading about the restaurant boom in your part of New Jersey, and we wanted in. My guy was young, just out of culinary school, and he was going somewhere, I knew all along."

"So you came looking in Grosvenor?"

"To tell you the truth, I wanted to find one in

Montclair. It's hotter than Grosvenor. But I couldn't touch anything there. The real estate is outta sight. The only place I could afford was Neon. I guess I shoulda done my homework better."

"You didn't know," Wally said.

"I tried to hold on after Frisco left. I made it two months, just using the sous chef and whoever she could find to help her. And then I threw in the towel. Even I wouldn't eat there."

"Too bad you couldn't hire Wade's old chef. He was pretty good, in my opinion."

"I tried," Barney said. "But he wouldn't come to me. I don't blame him. No one wants to take such a humiliating step down within earshot of the old place."

Wally saw in her rear-view mirror that someone was waiting for her parking space and didn't look happy about how long it was taking for Wally to move the car. She had to finish the call. "Do you know where he went?"

"Not a clue. He probably found something else, though, if he was as good as you say."

Wally intended to find out about that. But first she wanted to see if there was anything else Barney could tell her. "Do you know of anyone who would want to kill Wade Fuller?"

"What did you say your name was again?" Barney asked.

"Wally Morris."

"Morris, huh? Are you related to that guy who got arrested for killing Fuller?"

"He's my husband. But he didn't do it."

"Lady, I don't know you from a hole in the wall. I'll take your word for it that your hubby is innocent, but I don't know who killed Fuller. I'm just glad someone did. It gives me good, what do those television shrinks call it? Closure."

There didn't seem to be much else Wally could get

from Barney, so she thanked him and hung up. He'd given her something to think about, anyway. There was at least one more person on her list. But questioning Wade's old chef, when her husband was accused of murdering his former boss, was going to be awkward, to say the least.

Chapter Seventeen

"You missed an interesting funeral," said Louise when she called later in the afternoon.

Wally had been so busy all morning getting the children in her class ready for the holidays that she completely forgot about it. "What do you mean?"

"The pastor was looking for something nice to say about Wade, but could only find platitudes. She was really embarrassed."

Wally had been to funerals like that—where no one had a good word to say about the deceased. "Who was there?"

"All the usual suspects," Louise said. "Oh, I didn't mean that. Well, Nate wasn't there, but he shouldn't be a suspect, so—"

"I get it," said Wally. "Don't worry about that. What impression did you get?"

"Other than that Wade never did one charitable thing that anyone could talk about?"

"He did all that community work," Wally pointed out.

"No one believes that was for anything other than self-promotion. I'm a member of the Chamber of Commerce, too, and he was only there to promote his business and himself. You know his efforts to bring more business into town by getting the performing arts center built, and even becoming president of the restaurant association, were only so he could look after his own interests."

Wally hadn't thought Louise knew so much about Wade. "Why didn't you ever mention this all to me?"

"Why would I? Nate knew all this stuff, too. So did Norman. We're all in the same civic organizations, for the most part."

"Okay, I get it. Were many people from the Chamber and the other organizations there at the funeral?"

"A lot of them were. And I swear many of them were working the network, not mourning the victim."

"Did you notice anything that could help us?"

"Well, Wade's wife, Marcella, was doing a good job of being strong. And she looked fabulous in a Dana Buchman suit with Prada shoes and a terrific hat." That seemed fitting to Wally, considering she was going to take over the restaurant. It was long past the time when Marcella Fuller should have given up wearing warm-up suits everywhere. They had not even been designer track suits, as Louise had pointed out, which would have gone at least marginally better with all the fancy jewelry Marcella always wore, they had been simple velour in winter and cotton in summer.

Louise continued. "His step-daughter, Devin, was dressed just as well, although she was wearing Tahari and Jimmy Choos. I don't think an emotion crossed her face. Wade's sister was a basket case and she looked like something out of a rag bag by comparison."

"Wanda?"

"Yes. They were twins, you know. And from what I heard, they were pretty wild in high school and have always stayed very close."

"That's hard to believe sometimes, considering she's Fred Neimeyer's wife. He and Wade couldn't have been more different."

"Maybe that's why she's his soon-to-be-ex."

Wally wished she could share some of the Neimeyer information with Louise, if only to thoroughly talk it out to see if it all made sense, but she couldn't say a word. "Was Fred there?"

"He was, but he sat way in the back of the church. Their little girl was with him. And I saw Dominique and some of the detectives from the county."

"Was there anyone there you wouldn't expect?"

Louise seemed to be thinking about that, or something, because she was quiet for a moment. "Well, I don't know everyone he ever knew, but of the people I know, no."

It took a second or two for Wally to make sense of Louise's response. Louise broke into her thoughts when she added, "He got a very respectful sendoff. The whole Chamber of Commerce was there, including some of the regional leaders. There were also some of Devin's friends there, from college as well as high school. I recognized several of them from the fencing team. They were freshmen when Michelle was a senior."

Wally was reasonably sure she wouldn't have recognized anyone. Mark, her youngest child, had been out of high school even longer than Louise's daughter. "That was nice of them to come to show support."

"I think a few of them had been with her when she got the news," Louise said. "Her boyfriend seemed more distressed than she was."

"Anyone I'd know?"

"No. He didn't go to school in town. But I think they had been seeing each other for a while. Maybe he had formed a relationship with Wade."

Wally wondered if that was something Dominique should be looking into, but decided that without more to go on she shouldn't bring it up. It wouldn't do to send Dominique off on any wild goose chases.

So far, nothing was giving Wally any good ideas. Every businessperson in town was at the funeral, but was one of them the reason the funeral was necessary? "Was anyone from the play there?"

"Doug Norton was there, and the Clarks, although they weren't sitting together. I guess it's true about them splitting up. Do you think it means anything?"

"Such as did one of them kill Wade and now the other one doesn't want to have anything to do with the guilty spouse?" Wally asked.

"It could have happened," Louise said. "By the way, a few other members of the cast were there, as well as Babbette, who sat in the back. Notably absent, if you are talking about the cast, were Lance and Courtney. But I guess that makes sense. Why would either one of them care?"

Wally had no answer for that. "Was any of Wade's staff there?"

"No. I understand they were at the restaurant cooking for the mourners after the burial. I thought about going to the cemetery so I could go to the restaurant afterward, but I didn't have that much time. I had to show a house at three. And I'm sorry, there really hasn't been an opportunity for me to talk to Marcella."

"Thanks so much for going," Wally said. "I know you're busy."

"I'd do anything to help you and Nate," Louise said. "Just let me know if there is something else, and I'm there. Norman too."

The emotion in her voice nearly choked Wally up. "I'll let you know."

#

Wally didn't have time to check on any more people all day on Thursday. As much as she wanted to, she first needed to take care of business. So right after school she went to the butcher to stock up for the next week and the holiday, and after lunch she went to the grocery store to refill her refrigerator and pantry. It was not as if there was no food in the house at all, but there wasn't anything that could be whipped into a normal dinner and normal was what Wally wanted right now.

She made sure to get some more yeast and bread flour.

It was the time of year when the challah dough was shaped into a round spiral, to signify continuity and the circle of the year. The Jewish New Year, which oddly started in the middle of the month, even on the Hebrew calendar, was, like most Jewish holidays, full of custom and symbolism, and challahs. Wally took the roundness and sweetness of the holiday traditions to heart and every year made at least three tube cakes for dessert to cover both the sweet and the circular symbols. Since apples and honey were a big part of the imagery, one cake was usually apple and one honey chiffon. The third was chosen by whatever whim possessed her the day she was baking.

For some reason she couldn't explain, Wally had gone to Livingston to shop, not Grosvenor. She had to ask herself if she was avoiding people because she didn't want to talk about the problems, or if it was true that she just wanted to get some things in Livingston that weren't available in town. She could make a case either way, but it only served to make her feel grumpy, since the extra driving had meant even less time for helping Nate.

She ended up getting caught in traffic on the way home. It wasn't a common occurrence, but the bridge on Northfield was being repaired and there was a detour. There were too many cars to turn in the direction she wanted, so Wally ended up going with the traffic through the little streets of several fifties-era developments. It gave her time to think and her mind went back to the theater and the rehearsals.

Had there been an invisible force fighting against the play? Had someone not wanted it to get produced? How could that have turned into someone wanting to murder Wade?

Wally thought about the producers, Darby and Nanette Granger, that older couple who dressed as if they lived in another time and funded many of the local arts events. Wally didn't know them at all, except by reputation, but maybe this was the time to try to change that. She'd need an introduction, though, and she wondered who might provide it.

But the most important thing to find, Wally thought, as she turned onto her own street, was someone who had seen Nate during the time Wade was being attacked under the stage at the performing arts center. Someone who had seen him elsewhere. Everyone knew Nate had dropped off supplies and the table for the bake sale, but no one had seen him, up until the moment before it was time for the curtain to go up. Wally had even been waiting for him, as everyone who passed her and said hello knew. And even when he did show up, he ducked out again for another few minutes, and he could have been anywhere.

She had not known where he was during that time, and she still didn't. It must have had something to do with Fred Neimeyer; otherwise Nate would have said where he was and cleared himself right away.

This had gone on too long, Wally decided. It was time to get someone who could really clear Nate. And it looked like that someone might be Fred.

#

At times like this it felt to Dominique as if the cubicle she shared with her partner, Ryan, was even tighter than usual.

Dominique was impatient with Ryan. As much as he had improved as a detective, he was still cowed by authority, whether it was from the captain, the assistant prosecutor, or the county inspectors. They were all putting pressure on him and Dominique to close the case. They, meaning Adarra Dane and Inspectors Davis and Brady, were cheerfully planning the case against Nate Morris. While Dominique felt certain that they would all end up with egg on their collective face, she did not want it to be at the expense of the Morrises and their peace of mind.

But Ryan was knuckling under, saying things such as

169

"Nate Morris won't or can't account for the missing time. It must mean that he killed Fuller."

"And hit a dear friend over the head and stuffed her, bound up, into that closet?"

"He didn't hit her hard enough to really hurt her," Ryan argued, "and didn't tie her all that tight."

"*He* didn't do it," Dominique stated. "I am positive. And if you don't want to be the one who is blamed when they figure out they were all wrong, then you'd better help me find out who really did it."

"Adarra Dane said--"

Dominique looked at her partner. "I'm sure she is an excellent attorney. But she needs a solid case and right now she doesn't have one. If we find the real killer, she'll probably be grateful. And if we find that person before she announces to the whole world that Nate Morris did it and it comes out that he didn't, she'll really be grateful. It's a win-win situation."

Her phone vibrated. Dominique looked at the caller's number and debated about whether to take the call. It was Wally Morris and she would want some answers. Then again, maybe she had some of her own.

"Dominique, I'm so glad you're available. I need some information."

Hopes dashed, Dominique told Wally to ask away.

"I need a timeline for Wade Fuller on the afternoon he was k—" The sound of a car horn had obliterated Wally's last word.

"I'm sorry, I didn't get that," Dominique said. "Where are you?"

"In my car. But don't worry, I'm pulled over at the curb. I said I want a time line for the afternoon Wade was killed."

"She wants a time-line," Dominique whispered to Ryan. He shrugged and pulled a hard copy out of his file.

"Okay," said Dominique, when she had it in front of

170

her. "If it's okay with you, I'm going to put you on speaker, so my partner can hear."

"I guess it's okay," said Wally, who seemed quite uncertain. Then again, Dominique felt awkward too, whenever she knew she was on speaker.

Wally cleared her throat. "Hi, Ryan."

"Hey, Mrs. Morris," he said.

Dominique could only hope that maybe her partner would have a little more reason to investigate if he heard the voice of the wife of the wrongly accused man. "He went to a restaurant association luncheon and returned at about three. Actually we know exactly what time it was, thanks to the information you got from Babbette Fay. He was in his office for two hours, making and receiving calls. We know who he spoke to, with the exception of two incoming calls, one which was made from a pay phone at the train station and one from within the theater."

"Can't you figure out who made those calls?" asked Wally. "Don't they have cameras in the train station?"

"We don't have an answer yet, but we are checking," Dominique said.

"The call from inside the theater could have been the one from the murderer," Wally reasoned, "luring him there. Did you check for fingerprints?"

Dominique groaned inwardly. Wally couldn't know how hard it might be to find the phone. The police department had faced this type of problem before. Bomb threats phoned into the high school and middle school were nearly impossible to trace. It was too easy to buy a disposable cell phone anywhere, make a call, and get rid of it. It could take weeks to track down the store where it was purchased, let alone find records, which might only be available from security tapes, which had their own limitations, before a lead was found.

"We're checking," was all Dominique could say. "Moving on, Mr. Fuller went to check with his chef, Frisco, at five, when the early-bird dinners were well under way. There was a bigger than usual crowd because of the show. He greeted guests and chatted with the regulars until seven. Then he went back to his office to dress for the opening. At least that's what his maître d' said he was doing. He was the one who brought him his suit."

"He was planning to go to the play?" Wally said. "I didn't know that. Why would he?"

"I don't know. Mrs. Fuller seemed to think her husband wanted to make sure nothing would go wrong that could damage the theater or its reputation. He once told her there had been a threat."

"I didn't know any of this," Wally exclaimed.

Dominique held her tongue. No one not associated with the investigation was supposed to know that. It had been kept out of the papers.

"Okay," Wally said, "I'm sorry. I know I'm putting you into a tough position."

"It's okay, just don't spread it around."

"I won't. Can we assume that one of those calls was from someone letting Wade in on a potential threat?"

"It could have been," said Dominique, with far more reserve. "We're definitely thinking it's related."

Wally was silent for a moment. Dominique began to hope the call was nearly over.

It wasn't. "Well, if you're checking," Wally said, "then let's keep going. What time did he leave for the theater?"

"His hostess said he left at seven-thirty."

"The play was supposed to start at eight," Wally said, obviously thinking aloud. "So there was only a half hour when . . ."

"When what?"Dominique asked.

"Okay, thanks for the information," said Wally. "Well, I have to go now. Let me know if anything else comes up."

#

Wally pulled away from the curb. The call to Dominique and her partner had given Wally some information, but none of it would clear Nate. During the time she was waiting for Nate to show up at the theater, when he was essentially missing in action, Wade was being killed. If the time lines seemed to Wally to converge, they must really be pointing the finger at Nate in the minds of the police.

He had been somewhere else, Wally was sure. But where, he still wouldn't tell her. And he had probably been on foot. His car, after all, was busy having things stolen out of it.

So where could he have been? She knew he wouldn't tell her, so she had to find someone who might have seen him and not realized how important that information was.

She turned the corner and found herself stuck in the five o'clock rush hour traffic of Grove Street. The four lane road narrowed to three with only one going east as it went into the center of town, inevitably causing a long back-up of cars as they jockeyed for position. Traffic on the cross streets got tied up when cars got stuck in the middle of the intersection. The result was a daily snarl. Wally had forgotten about that when she made the turn. Now she'd have a while to consider how to clear Nate.

Her mind went back to the problem at hand. If she didn't know where Nate had gone, how was she to find someone who might have seen him? People didn't just stand around outside watching things. They all had their own business, their own lives and their own agendas. But if she could figure out where he'd gone during the time between when he left his car in the parking lot of the theater and when he came in just before the performance, maybe she could find someone who had seen him.

She tried to calculate how far he might have gone on foot in the fifteen to twenty minutes he was unaccounted for. He was a fast walker, so he could have gone just about anywhere from the university to the house to the high school. Within that radius was the whole town, the homes of all their friends, the business district, and the county park reservation, full of walking trails and paths with spectacular views of New York City.

It seemed unlikely that was where Nate had gone. When he came in he wasn't even winded, so he must have been closer to the theater. Wally thought about what was nearby.

Marcella's, Wade's restaurant, jumped to the front of her mind. But why would Nate have gone there?

She tried to think of alternate places he might have gone but none made sense. If he had been somewhere else, someone they knew would have seen him and come forward to exonerate.

But Marcella's was at the edge of the business district, past the bridge over the creek. The only structures nearby were the two businesses across the street and the church on the corner. But who might have seen Nate, if he'd been there at all, that evening?

Wally looked for the nearest side street, drove up it, and parked. She took out her phone again and speed dialed Nate's cell.

"Hi," he said. "What's up?"

His breezy manner irritated Wally. Here she was agonizing over clearing his name and he was casually going about his day without a care in the world. Maybe there wasn't anything he could do about his case right now, but even so, shouldn't he have some anxiety?

"I'll tell you what's up, Nate Morris," she said. "I have been trying to find a way to get your named cleared and the biggest obstacle has been you. I need you to tell me where you were that evening so I can find someone who saw you there."

"You know I can't do that without implicating

174

someone in something else," he told her.

"Why are you willing to go to jail for Fred Neimeyer? What did he ever do for you?"

"I'm not going to jail. If it comes to that, I'm sure he, er, someone will step up."

Wally felt herself losing patience. "I'm not willing to wait any longer. I am your wife and I want you to tell me where you were so I can find someone to corroborate your alibi. If I can get someone other than Fred, fine, but I'm not making any guarantees."

Nate was silent and Wally gripped the phone, willing it to speak to her.

"Okay," he said, "I'll tell you this much. We were in the vicinity of Marcella's. But I didn't see anyone. I couldn't even see the street most of the time, so I don't know how I could be seen. That's all I have to say."

Wally started to ask him what he meant but realized he was no longer on the line. It didn't sound promising, and didn't make sense, but it did confirm her theory. She quickly got out of the car and ran back up the block, over the bridge and into Blossoms.

"Hi, Wally," Fergie said. "What can I do for you today?"

"I was hoping . . ." Wally stopped. It seemed too easy. If Fergie had seen Nate that afternoon, wouldn't she have mentioned that to the police? But there was nothing to lose by asking, except maybe another thin ray of hope. "I wondered if you had seen Nate on the evening Wade was killed. Maybe across the street?"

Fergie looked out her window at the restaurant. "I thought you'd be trying to help Nate."

"I am."

"Then why would you want me to confirm he was at the victim's place of business?"

"Because then he couldn't have been at the theater. Did you see him there?"

Fergie stared wide-eyed at Wally. "You're looking for an alibi in the place where Wade worked? If he were there would it be a good alibi or would it look like he was looking for Wade to . . ."

Wally sucked in her breath. Fergie had a point. "Sorry I bothered you," Wally said.

"I guess he could have been there," Fergie said. "I don't spend my days looking out the window."

"Thanks for the encouragement," Wally said. "I won't waste anymore of your time."

She went outside. Long shadows made it dark on the street. It matched her mood.

The only other business across from the restaurant was the ballet school. It was empty now, but Wally wondered, for a brief, desperate moment, if there were classes on Friday evenings.

She'd have to come back tomorrow and see. Maybe someone had seen Nate. In the meantime she was going to work on Nate, to see if she could get anything out of him. He must have had a good reason to be late to the theater. And it must have involved Fred or Nate would have been defending himself to anyone who would listen. He was still hiding whatever Fred had been up to that evening. It couldn't have been a murder, since Nate wouldn't protect anyone who had committed a crime, but it was obviously something.

Wally had to wonder just how bad it had been. There was nothing she could do to figure that out, but she could try to figure out what he meant when he said he couldn't see the street. Had he been inside the restaurant? People in there would have seen him.

She looked at her watch. The early birds would be gone by now and the people who wanted to catch dinner and a movie would be mid-meal. It was late and she should be home, but she had made no progress toward clearing Nate. She had to try again. As there were more people to talk to, she crossed over to the restaurant and went inside.

"Will you be having dinner?" asked the maître d'.

"Not today," Wally said. "I wondered, though, if I might have a word with your chef."

"And why would you want to do that, Mrs. Morris?" asked a voice. Wally turned and found Marcella Fuller, dressed today in a black knit dress which clung to her curves and whose décolletage was only covered by a large, square-cut emerald necklace.

Wally cleared her throat. Perhaps she hadn't thought this through, but there was nothing to do but go ahead and do the right thing. That began with an offer of condolences. Hopefully it would not sound like an admission of any kind. "I am so sorry for your loss," she said.

"That means nothing, coming from the wife of the man who killed him," Marcella snarled. "How can you come in here and face me?"

"I have nothing to be ashamed of," Wally told her. "Nate did not do this horrible thing. It would be a mistake to let the real killer go free, just because the police suspect the wrong man."

"That's your version. Now, before I throw you out of here, tell me what you want."

"I just wanted to talk to your chef for a moment."

"Are you booking a function? Because if you are not, there is no reason for the two of you to speak. Unless, that is, you suspect him of killing Wade."

Wally was not enjoying this conversation, but she was in too deep to let it go without looking like she was skulking out with her tail between her legs. "Do you?"

"Why would he? He has a great new job at a much higher salary."

"Then why wonder about him?" Wally asked.

"Forget it. Please leave."

Wally walked out of the restaurant with her head held

high, willing herself to keep her body language neutral so that she wouldn't look as if she was leaving with her tail between her legs. The image of that almost made her laugh and she thought the story would entertain her best friend. And that gave her another idea.

As soon as she was out the door Wally called Louise. "Meet me at Marcella's," she said. "We need a drink."

"If you want something, you can come over here," Louise suggested.

"No," Wally corrected her. "We need it at Marcella's."

"I'll be right there."

Louise must have caught the sense of adventure in Wally's voice because she arrived minutes later wearing a conspiratorial smile. "What's this about?"

"I want Marcella to know I'm watching her. She won't let me talk to her chef and she asked me to leave the restaurant if I wasn't doing business there, so I want to give her the business, so to speak."

Louise looked at Wally in surprise. "I've never known you to be vindictive."

Wally sighed. "I'm really not trying to give her a hard time. I'd rather make friends with her, so she'll let me talk to the chef. What better way than over a glass of wine?"

Marcella's eyebrows rose when Wally walked back into the restaurant. She seemed to gird herself for a confrontation, but relaxed when she saw Louise. She replaced her frown with a rigid smile.

"You must have some clout," Wally whispered. "Marcella pulled in her claws when she saw you."

"She probably wouldn't want me to tell new homeowners that the restaurant is bad." Louise gave Marcella a big grin. It brought the woman over and she set them up with a table and two menus.

"Maybe we'd better get some appetizers, too," Wally said from behind her menu. She didn't want to be rude.

She just wanted to find a way to get the information she needed.

"I'm game."

The waiter came over and asked for their drink orders. Once that was done, Wally found that making small talk with Louise, usually the easiest thing in the world, was difficult under these circumstances. She absolutely could not talk about the things which were most important.

Louise picked up the slack when their glasses of wine were delivered. "I just got another listing."

"Oh," said Wally, only half listening. The other half of her brain was trying to figure out how to ask Marcella again for permission to talk to the chef. "That's great. Do you think it will be an easy sale?"

"If they stage it right, I hope it will."

Wally's eyes flicked over to Marcella and then back to Louise. "Stage?"

"You know. When you make the house look like the ones on the home renovation shows on television."

"Right." Wally looked at Marcella again.

"It does need work, though," Louise admitted. "That will have to be done first."

"Of course," Wally agreed. She took another sip of her wine and realized that in her nervousness she had consumed the whole glass. If she wasn't careful, she would be on the curb again in seconds. "Oops. Maybe we should order."

Louise laughed. "Norman will be on his own for dinner, I guess."

By the time they'd finished eating their seared tuna with wasabi risotto garnish appetizers, which were really enough for a whole meal, Wally had relaxed. She hadn't figured out what to do about her problem with Marcella, but she was feeling calmer, even though she'd switched to ginger ale. Louise was telling her a story about her daughter who was away in graduate school and living in an apartment alone for the first time. The story involved a mouse in a kitchen, a sturdy door, and many takeout dinners with paper plates.

Wally was mid-laugh when a disgusted looking Marcella came over.

"The tuna appetizer is fabulous," Wally said. Louise, whose mouth was full, nodded in agreement. "Does it come as a full dinner?"

Marcella's shoulders lost some of their rigidness. "Yes. Were you thinking of coming in for dinner? We've been very busy, so I'd recommend a reservation." Her tone was only slightly less icy, but she seemed to be reevaluating her position.

"We will definitely be back," Louise promised.

With a sigh, Marcella said "I'll give you one minute with the chef. Then I'd appreciate it if you'd give up this table. There are people waiting."

"I'll meet you outside," Wally told Louise.

While Louise paid the bill, Wally hurried in the direction of the kitchen, hoping it was still in the same location it had been during the other incarnations of the restaurant. She passed a familiar looking busboy, one whom she was sure used to work for Telly's, but he did not meet her gaze. Wade, when he expanded, had taken more from Telly, including personnel, than Wally had realized.

She pushed open the door and spotted Frisco, standing in the back talking to one of the sous chefs. Since she only had one minute, she hurried over and introduced herself.

"Spare the rage," she said when she saw Frisco's face contort in anger. "My husband didn't do it."

As Frisco opened his mouth, she put up her hand. "I don't think you did either. I just wanted to find out if you know where the former chef is. No one seems to be able to find him."

"Why didn't you ask Marcella? She'd have his home address."

"He moved, according to the police. Please, do you know how I can find him?"

"Why don't you try the restaurant association? He'd be listed there if he ever wants to get another job. They have placement services."

"Thanks," Wally said. "I'll give it a try."

Frisco had calmed considerably. "Do the police think he did it?"

"They just want to talk to him. He may know who was sufficiently angry with Wade to kill him."

Her minute was up and she could see Marcella heading toward the kitchen, so she quickly scooted out the back door into the alley. After all that bargaining with Marcella, not to mention the wine and tuna, she hadn't really learned anything useful.

She stopped suddenly. Had this been where Nate was on the night of the murder, while he was busy not being visible from the street? It was possible, she supposed, but she couldn't think of why he'd have been there.

A noise behind her made her jump. She turned and saw the busboy, Alberto, formerly of Telly's.

He ducked behind a dumpster. Intrigued by his odd behavior, Wally pursued him. Alberto seemed startled to see her, and hid his hand, which obviously held a cigarette, behind his back.

"I didn't mean to scare you," she said. When he wouldn't look at her, she started to go, but stopped. "Is something wrong?"

"What do you mean?"

"You seem to be hiding."

"I am not allowed to smoke on break. I could get fired. Please don't tell."

"I won't say anything." Wally waited. His uneasiness did not diminish. "Is there something else?"

Alberto looked around. "I don't know if I should say anything, but I saw your husband here, that night. Outside

181

the kitchen door."

Almost afraid to hear the answer, Wally said, "What was he doing?"

"He was arguing with a man. I've seen him too."

"What did they do?"

"The man went inside, into Mr. Fuller's office. Your husband tried to stop him."

"Did he go inside too?"

Alberto looked frightened.

"You can tell me."

"No. He was out here."

"Why didn't he see you?"

"I was back here, behind the dumpster."

"Do you remember what time that was?"

"Seven-thirty-five, when I went on break. Maybe a few minutes later. He was here until I finished. When he finally left, I hurried back inside."

Wally did the math in her mind, and felt certain that would put Nate here, or on his way to the theater, at the time of the actual attack on Wade. "Could you testify to that?"

He looked at her as if she had lost her mind. "You don't understand. I didn't say anything because I don't want to get fired. I was not supposed to be smoking."

Wally felt like she was about to explode. Fred Neimeyer was doing something wrong so he couldn't come forward, and the one other person who could clear Nate was worried about his job. "I'll make sure you can go back to Telly's if that happens," she promised, struggling to hide her anger. "And you don't have to say what anyone was doing; just that Nate was here, and at what time." She wondered if the police would let it go at that. It wouldn't do to clear Nate of murder and then have him be caught in Fred's mishegoss--his crazy problems.

"I don't know."

"Do you want to see an innocent man go to jail?"

182

Wally was having trouble controlling her emotions. Tears were threatening. "While a murderer goes free?"

Alberto shook his head. "I will do it. You're a nice lady. I want to help you and Mr. Morris, too."

Chapter Eighteen

After a sleepless night waiting to hear that Nate's witness had come forward, Wally felt as if she were dragging all morning. The children were more excited than they had been earlier in the week, but that wasn't uncommon. Fridays were the day that Shabbat was celebrated in the nursery school, even though technically it didn't start until sundown. Apple juice and challah with cream cheese and cut up fruit had the expected effect on the children. Wally did her best to keep up.

Rachel and her children were coming for the weekend to show their support, an idea that seemed to have originated with Nate, who was still trying to avoid confirming Wally's theory about the reason for his being at the restaurant. Wally stopped at the fruit market to stock up before going home to get to work on her challah dough and a pareve chocolate cake for Rachel's birthday. It had cheered Wally somewhat that Rachel still wanted her mother's cake for her birthday, and made having to put a front on for the grandchildren more tolerable.

But it was really worrisome how Debbie and Elliot would also have to hide their feelings. They weren't angry at each other, Wally knew, but Debbie was under a lot of pressure and Elliot was helpless as to how to get her through it. Since he hadn't managed to turn anything up, he hadn't been able to make her feel better.

The phone was ringing when Wally got home and she picked it up just after Nate answered from his office. It was the house line, but he must have thought she hadn't come in yet.

Debbie was on the line, sounding as excited as she had the day she got into college. "I just got a call from Dominique. She said the charges against you will be dismissed."

"So it's over?" said Nate, sounding as if he could barely believe it.

Wally was thrilled but wanted to savor the details. "Did the assistant prosecutor accept the witness' statement?"

"Yes," said Debbie. "And yes. She did have a few questions about why you were there, though, Dad."

Nate didn't say anything. Then again, Debbie hadn't asked. Wally got the message.

"Does Elliot know?" Nate asked, breaking the awkward silence.

"I already called him. He is delighted."

As the realization sunk in with Wally, a flood of relief washed over her. "I'll see you both at dinner later," she said. "I know we'll have big appetites for a change."

#

Debbie and Elliot, holding hands, left right after they finished their cake. Wally didn't mind at all.

#

The observance of the Shabbat day of rest at synagogue the next day, made so much more significant by all the work Wally had done that crazy week, was uplifting. Jodi and Charlie were the center of attention among Wally and Nate's group at the Kiddush following services. A long, lazy afternoon playing with the grandchildren topped off the day.

Even Wally's Sunday chores didn't dampen her mellow mood. Doing the laundry, preparing for the coming holidays and her students' projects for the week, went smoothly. When Nate suggested dinner out, Wally's perfect weekend was complete. She felt so much better that she decided to make dinner for the first evening of Rosh Hashanah and invited everyone.

"Nate," she said, after she finished issuing invitations, "could you just tell me one thing?"

He looked up from the book he was reading. "I will if I can."

She'd have to live with that. "You said you knew Fred didn't murder Wade. But how can you be sure he didn't do it after you were with him at the restaurant?"

Nate seemed to be thinking. "I don't think there would have been any way. I don't think he knew Wade was at the theater, and even if he did, how would Fred have had time to get him down to the basement? Fred wasn't anywhere near my car, as far as I know, so he couldn't have taken my cap and those other things."

That was certainly not the strongest alibi Wally had ever heard. "Where was he when you last saw him?"

"He was sitting at Starbucks, drinking black coffee. Or at least that was what I sent him in there to do. I couldn't tell for sure what he was having when I looked through the window."

"Are you saying he was drunk?"

"Maybe not legally. But enough to do something crazy like try to get into Wade's office without permission."

"So he has an alibi. Too bad you didn't go in with him so you could have one too."

"I was hurrying back into the theater to see my lovely wife."

Wally wasn't letting him off the hook so easily, notwithstanding his charm. "Which time? You came in twice, remember?"

"The second time. I told Fred to go get coffee and went into the theater. Then I decided to make sure Fred was following my instructions, so I ran out again. It only took a minute to check on him and then I was back for good."

Wally's annoyance at the situation, frustratingly pent up for so long, threatened to spill out all over Nate. "Someone must have seen you together near Starbucks, and you knew it. We could have found that person and you would have had an alibi." She held up her hand, to stop Nate from speaking. "I know. We couldn't say anything because it might cast a light of suspicion on Fred." She sighed. "I'll get over it. I'm just glad you were cleared."

But Monday morning brought fresh reminders that the murder case was still open and the investigation ongoing. Dominique left Wally a message on her cell phone asking her to spare a few minutes after school to come into the police station.

When she arrived Wally got the sense that there was an air of frustration between Dominique and Ryan. "Davis?" Wally asked.

"Who else?" Dominique sighed. "He wasn't pleased that we don't have any leads. So I was hoping . . ."

When she didn't finish her sentence, Wally knew she was in for a long afternoon. "What can I do?"

"We want to take you back to the theater, to see if there is anything else you can remember."

Wally looked from Dominique to Ryan. She had no choice but to agree.

Davis was in the theater when they arrived and Brady came in a few minutes later. If it hadn't been so serious, Wally probably would have been laughing, as all eyes turned to her. She'd have to pull something out of her brain, something she hadn't mentioned before, maybe because she was afraid it would implicate Nate, or they would all be wasting their time.

The set was still there, untouched. "They were about to strike it," Dominique explained. "That's why we needed you to come today."

Carefully looking it over, Wally didn't notice anything. "It all looks the same to me."

"Nothing is jogging your memory?"

"Not really. The chair is just where it was when Wade was on it, the other furniture hasn't been moved, and the skimpy excuse for flower arrangements is still just as inadequate as ever."

Dominique turned surprised eyes toward Wally. "What does that mean?"

Wally shook her head. "It's nothing against Fergie. I'm sure if the flowers had been arranged properly they would have been lovely. We had planned for that while we were working on the sets, not putting in too much color because the flowers were supposed to add it. But whoever did them must have been in a big rush or just didn't care how they looked. It was a shame. Of course, Wade getting murdered was a bigger one."

"What is she talking about?" Davis growled. "I thought you said she might be able to help. All she seems to care about is a bunch of flowers."

"I'm sorry," Wally said. "I'm sure it isn't important."

Dominique shook her head. "Hold on a minute. It could be important. Do you know why the flowers weren't arranged properly?"

"Fergie wasn't able to get here in time to put them out herself. She had to call someone and ask to have them put out for her. Maybe the person didn't realize he was supposed to mix them and make them look like bouquets. Or maybe he didn't know how."

"Do you know who that was?"

Wally didn't remember whether Fergie had mentioned it. But it didn't seem important. She shrugged.

Davis was about to open his mouth when Ryan darted up the aisle of the theater. "I'll find out," he said over his shoulder.

"Can you think of anything else?" Dominique asked.

188

"Nothing here. Maybe we should go backstage."

"Lead the way, Mrs. Morris," Davis said. He seemed surlier than usual, but maybe it was just because he was embarrassed about thinking Nate was the murderer. Or maybe it was because they were starting from square one, over a week after the murder.

Wally went up onto the stage and into the wing. "Everything seems to be the same as when I was working on the sets, with the exception of Babbette's omnipresence." During the weeks before the play it had seemed as if Babbette was there twenty-four seven. "She was late arriving that night, or she might have met the same fate as Louise."

"Did we know that?" asked Davis, making a note.

"Yes," said Dominique. "And I called the ballet school to confirm that Babbette had picked up her daughter at the same time as the murder."

Babbette's name was crossed off. Davis's disgusted look returned.

Brady looked around. "Is this all there is backstage?"

"There's a bit more." Wally led them all to the behind the stage area and out the back entrance to the alley behind the theater where she and Babbette had worked on the sets. Wally explained about Wade's rule that no painting could be done inside the theater.

"It's amazing what you created considering the obstacles you had to overcome," Dominique said.

"It was all Babbette, believe me. I just did what she said."

"Where does that driveway lead?" Brady asked, indicating a strip of blacktop on the far end of the theater.

"To Grove Avenue. These stores and the apartments above them which are opposite us," Dominique pointed, "are all on Grove. They back up onto this alley, and the people who live in them drive up the alley to park. They can go up their back stairs, as you can see."

As if he didn't believe her, Brady lumbered his large body over to the driveway and had a look. He nodded his head and started back to where the rest of the group was standing.

Before he reached them, Ryan came out with a young man. "He's the one who put out the flowers," Ryan said.

"How did you know that you had to do the flowers?" Dominique asked after telling him who she was.

"Someone called me."

"Who?" Davis asked, without introducing himself.

The man shrugged. "It sounded like the lady who dropped them off that morning. She told me she would come back during the day to set them up."

"What did she say when she called before the show?"

"Not much. She sounded out of breath and said she couldn't do it herself. So she asked me to put them into the vases."

"Did she say why she couldn't get there?" Davis asked.

"Not really. Just that she couldn't. I told her I'd do it, she said thanks and she hung up." He looked puzzled. "They weren't real flowers, you know. Did I do something wrong?"

"No," said Dominique. "But we may need to take your statement, so we'll need some information."

As Dominique collected the man's numbers, Wally started to think that the police were looking at Fergie. "You can't think Fergie Schultz did it," she said to Dominique as soon as they were out of earshot of the others.

"We have to check it out. What do you know about her?"

Wally bit her lip. "She told me in confidence," she said.

Dominique waited. The look on her face said that she was expecting Wally to divulge the information.

"She had an affair with Wade. It ended badly and it was affecting her business. But she isn't the type to--"

"Let us do our work," Dominique said, looking energized. "If she didn't do it, there won't be any problems."

"I'm sure it must be someone else," Wally said. "If I have to find that person myself, I'll do it. I don't want to be responsible for Fergie getting into trouble."

"Thanks for coming," was Dominique's only response. She went to rejoin the other members of the investigation, leaving Wally to worry once again.

Chapter Nineteen

"You've got to do something," said Martha Knight when she called Wally the next day. "They've brought my niece in for questioning. Belle is going crazy."

Wally hadn't heard the news, but that didn't surprise her. The police were not releasing any information about Fergie or the case until they had checked every angle. If they couldn't find evidence against the florist, they would just let her leave.

Or so Wally sincerely hoped. She was still feeling guilty for Fergie even being considered as a suspect. "Tell your sister not to worry so much about her daughter. Fergie will just explain where she was at the time Wade Fuller was killed, and that will be that."

"I hope you're right, Wally," said Martha. "I'm not in a position to help Fergie myself, you know."

"How is the rehab going?" Wally asked, hoping to deflect the conversation from the subject of Martha's niece.

"Slow. You know what they say, young bones heal quickly, old bones . . . well, you must know."

Wally wasn't going to touch that one. Martha was at least fifteen years older than she. Martha's equating Wally with herself, age-wise, must have been the stress addling her brain.

"You know what makes me almost as mad as them arresting Fergie? That they haven't even tried to find out who nearly ran me down."

"Sure they did," said Wally, before she could stop

herself. She was reasonably sure Dominique wouldn't like her talking about it. But she knew they had run all the motor vehicle records in the area for all-white vans, but they hadn't drawn any conclusions.

"You'd think they'd really want to know," Martha said, "since Mr. Fuller was standing right there. It might even have been an attempt on his life."

"That's very good thinking," said Wally, especially since she'd been thinking the same thing all along. "I'm sure the police are looking into it."

"You should call them."

"Who?"

"The police. Or your son-in-law. He'll know who to tell."

"Okay," Wally promised. A reminder call, maybe not to Elliot, but to Dominique, couldn't hurt. Martha seemed happy with that and let Wally "get right to it."

But maybe it would be better just to find out who could have killed Wade. Wally had already done a lot of legwork, this would just be a matter of picking it back up. Then again, she didn't exactly have much time, not with everything she had to do.

On the other hand, after being the one to implicate Fergie, it was the least she could do.

    #

"Restaurant Association, this is Gloria, may I help you?"

"I hope so, Gloria." Wally said into the phone, while picturing a woman in an office somewhere with direct access to the best restaurants in New Jersey. "I'm trying to find Rocco Paradis. He is a chef who left his previous employer and I was hoping to get in touch with him."

"Is this about a job?"

"Not exactly. I just wanted to talk to him."

"I'm sorry," said Gloria. "It is not our policy to give out information to just anyone who asks."

"Please, it's important. It might be a matter of life and death."

The silence on the other end of the phone line led Wally to believe that the woman was somewhat skeptical. Her tone when she spoke confirmed it. "You'll have to give me more than that," said Gloria.

Her voice said 'curious,' not 'I'm calling 911,' so Wally told her the whole story about how Wade was murdered and it was important to find out who did it. "We can't overlook any possible suspects," Wally concluded. "If they take the wrong person to trial, it will only give the murderer more time to cover his tracks."

Gloria conceded the point. "I'll give you his cell phone number as soon as I look it up. Sorry, but my computer is slow, and I haven't even turned it on yet. This could take a while."

"No problem," said Wally. "I can wait." This was a golden opportunity, she thought. With any luck, this woman would talk to fill the time and maybe Wally could learn something.

She wasn't disappointed. "Don't you people think that he's likely to tell you he wasn't anywhere near the scene of the crime?" Gloria said.

By "you people" Wally took it that Gloria thought she was with the police, although she hadn't said anything close to that or even spoken with an official tone. "We, I mean I, just want to ask him a few questions. I'm not making any accusations."

"I doubt he'll talk to you," Gloria said. "I don't even know if he's planning to stay around here. If I were him, I'd be looking in another state."

"Why do you say that?"

Gloria snorted. "Because of what happened at the northern Jersey luncheon. Come to think of it, that was the same day Mr. Fuller was killed."

Wally could feel her heart beat faster. "What

194

happened?"

"Oh, it was awful," said Gloria. "Mr. Fuller was talking to a bunch of other restaurant owners when Rocco asked if he could talk to him for a minute. Mr. Fuller--. Oh here we go. Do you have a pencil?"

"What?"

"I have that number for you. Do you still want it?"

"Oh, yes."

Gloria rattled off the number. "Good luck," she said.

"WAIT!" Wally said, entirely too loudly, but she was afraid Gloria would hang up without finishing her story. "Don't hang up."

"I beg your pardon?"

"You were telling me what happened at the luncheon."

"Oh, that's right. I nearly forgot."

Wally shook her head in puzzlement. How could someone forget—?

"Mr. Fuller looked at Rocco and seemed annoyed. He turned to the other owners and said "Remember this guy. If you see him coming, lock your doors. He's a terrible chef.""

"Why would Wade do that?"

"Who knows? He could sometimes be pretty mean." That statement, said with a catch in Gloria's voice, seemed to Wally to be from the voice of experience.

"Do you think the other restaurant owners were likely to believe what Wade said?"

"I don't know. But if I were Rocco, I'd have been mighty embarrassed. And I'd be worried about whether or not I'd ever find a new job."

Worried enough to kill Wade to keep him from bad mouthing Rocco any further? Wally didn't think that likely, but then again, the alternative, suspecting poor little Fergie, was also unthinkable.

Wally didn't waste any time punching the numbers into her phone. She was just rehearsing what to say when the call answering feature came on. She had no choice but to leave a message. It was unlikely Rocco would call back, but she could be persistent.

#

It was just after one o'clock on Wednesday and Wally was deep into the kneading process for her round challahs for the holiday when the phone rang. She wiped the sticky dough off her fingers and grabbed for the receiver.

"Is this the lady who called me?" asked a voice. Wally immediately knew who he was.

"Rocco. Thanks for returning my call." Wally wondered what she could possibly say that the police wouldn't have asked, something that would miraculously reveal the true killer.

"What can I do for you?" the man said, somewhat impatiently. "Is this about Fuller's murder? Is everyone in your area code investigating?"

"Have you had a lot of calls?" Wally asked, obviously unnecessarily.

"Just you and everybody else."

"You mean other than the police?"

"The police," he said, "Wade's wife, his daughter, er, step-daughter, which is a lucky thing for her."

"Lucky? In what way?"

"That he wasn't her real dad and so she couldn't have inherited his genes for mean."

Wally had the urge to laugh out loud or at least award kudos to Rocco for his little rhyme, but this wasn't the time. "Anyone else?"

"His brother-in-law. And, um, oh, no forget that."

"Who?" Wally prodded.

"No one," Rocco said quickly. "Is there anything else you want to ask me?" He seemed even more anxious to get off the phone.

"Actually, yes. What did those people, other than the police of course, want from you?"

'Well, let's see. Which one?"

196

Wally took out some paper and a pen. Her dough was going to have to wait. "Let's start with Wade's wife, Marcella. What did she want?"

"She wanted to know if I murdered Wade." Rocco said. "I told her no."

"Can you prove that?"

"I was on my way to the Hamptons for the weekend. I had a houseful of witnesses who saw me arrive at eight, so I couldn't have been in Grosvenor when Wade was killed. Unless you think I can fly."

"Why do you think Marcella suspected you?"

"I'm not entirely sure," Rocco told Wally. "I had the feeling she was hoping I did because she was afraid of who it might have been."

Wally was momentarily at a loss for words. "Who did she think might have done it?"

"She didn't actually say. But there are only two people she ever cared about and one was dead."

"Devin? Did she think her daughter did it?"

"Do you think she'd tell me that?"

"I suppose not," Wally conceded. "Okay, so then you said you talked to Devin. What did she say?"

"At first she thanked me but I told her I couldn't take credit. Sure, I wasn't too upset when I heard he had been killed, but I didn't really want the guy dead."

"Even after what he said at the restaurant association luncheon?"

"Oh, you heard about that. He and I came to terms afterward. I'm sure I could have gotten a good recommendation out of him. I thought I needed it, but maybe I didn't, after all."

"Oh, did you find a new job?"

"I'm waiting to hear. But I think so."

"Congratulations. You said at first Devin thanked you."

"Yeah. It almost made me want to take credit. She

had a horrible relationship with Wade. She used to complain about him to me when she was catching an after-school snack on her way home."

"When you told her you didn't do it, what did Devin say?"

"She asked me who I thought did it. She went from being relaxed to being kind of nervous, but I don't know why. And since I don't have a clue who did it, I really couldn't make her feel any better."

"What did Wade's brother-in-law, Fred Neimeyer, want?"

"He just wanted to make sure I didn't, and these are his words, 'misinterpret any altercations' he had with Wade. I told him I really had no idea what he was talking about."

"Did you ever hear them fighting?"

"All the time. Usually on the phone. Wade's office was next to the kitchen, and Wade would tell Fred that he had better do what Wanda wanted or else. I don't know what that was."

Wally did, or at least she knew what Nate had told her about Fred and Wanda's marital disputes, the extortion, spearheaded by Wade, and the threats.

"There was one more person you mentioned," Wally said. "What did that person say to you?"

"Who?"

"The other person who called you."

"Um, no. Forget what I said. There was no one else. Just the police. Someone named Dominique Scott." His tone said he wasn't saying any more about the calls.

Wally was disappointed that she hadn't been able to find out who Rocco was protecting. It could potentially be important, but, although they spoke for another few minutes, she learned nothing else.

After she hung up, she hurried to finish kneading her dough to get it ready to rise. She had to place each of the two batches of dough, the plain one and the raisin one, into greased bowls and cover them with plastic wrap to let them rise in a warm place. Today her entire kitchen was a warm place. But it was nothing compared to the hot water she'd accidentally gotten Fergie Schultz into with her big mouth.

She readied the rest of the evening's dinner to be cooked, setting out the necessary pots and pans. There wasn't a chance to make any of the calls she itched to make for another few minutes. The good thing, though, was that there seemed to be several leads left to follow, and hopefully she could find the one that would clear Fergie.

But she couldn't help wondering if maybe Nate had been wrong all along and Fred Neimeyer had been the one to slit Wade Fuller's throat. Had he lured Wade to the basement area of the theater and killed him? That phone call, the one Wade received from a blocked number, might have been the reason Wade had changed his mind and decided to go to the theater that evening. It was well known that Wade had a big stake in the theater and the murderer could have planned to find him there. But maybe the murderer had not wanted to leave anything to chance, so he called Wade and said there was a problem.

What would that person have said? Wally tried to imagine. Maybe if she could figure that out, she would have some idea of who might have been the caller. Would the person have said someone else wanted him there? Then he would have wondered why the person didn't place the call. If that were true, then the person had to be someone who had something to do with the theater, or at least a reason to be there. But the police had eliminated all those suspects.

Wally wondered why Devin had called Rocco. She wondered if there was any way to talk to the girl. A glance at the clock told her that Devin's mother, Marcella, was likely to be at the restaurant at this time of day. It would be a good time to try to reach the girl at home. If not, Wally could try to get her number at the college.

Devin answered the phone right away. Wally introduced herself and explained that she had wanted to offer condolences to the family right after Wade's passing, but that under the circumstances while Nate was a suspect, it would have been too awkward.

"Thanks," said Devin.

"The police have a suspect," Wally told her.

"Who?"

"I'd rather not say. But I don't think that person killed your father."

"Step-father," Devin corrected her. "Wade was not my father."

"Yes, sorry. I wondered if maybe you could help get the right person to pay for the crime. Do you have any idea who might have wanted your, um, Wade dead?"

"I can think of a few people. Wade's brother-in-law yelled at him a lot. And I've heard his old chef yelling too. And there were other people." She paused before rushing on. "But he didn't do it."

"Who?"

"My boyfriend. He hated Wade, I'll admit it, but he wouldn't do such a thing."

"I'm sure that's easy to prove," Wally said in a comforting voice. "Where was he at the time?"

"He went home for the weekend. You could call his mother to check."

It was more likely that Wally would call Dominique and have her check, but Wally didn't mention that. She was feeling a little stupid and unfeeling for continuing to talk to this child.

"Okay," she said. "Was there anyone else? Anyone who might have had some business with Wade? Something about the new theater?"

"Oh, yes," said Devin. "There was one, no, two other people. Mr. and Mrs. Granger. I remember that the Grangers called him several times the week he was killed and they left a lot of messages."

That was a surprise. Wally knew they had a big stake in the theater and had given a large chunk of cash to get it started, but she couldn't imagine what the problem might have been at that point in the construction phase and in getting the theater ready to open. "Did they say what they wanted?"

"No. I just took their number down and left it for Wade. They didn't want his number at work, though, which I offered, so I guess they had it."

It made Wally wonder. "Thanks for talking to me," she said. "And please tell your mother that I am truly sorry for her loss."

After she hung up she immediately called Dominique and told her about her phone call with Devin. "Did you talk to Devin's boyfriend?"

"He has an alibi."

"Okay." Wally knew she was getting nowhere following this line of questioning. "Have you been able to question Harvey Floyd?"

"He hasn't regained consciousness. It doesn't look good. The smoke inhalation was extensive. The doctors aren't giving up, though."

"But you must have some idea of who set the fire, or something."

"Wow, Wally, slow down," said Dominique. "What's gotten into you?"

"Sorry. Martha begged me to help clear Belle's daughter. I think it's only fair, since something I said made you suspect her. Did you find any evidence?" Wally asked, knowing she was going to get an unsatisfactory answer.

She also knew she shouldn't even be asking, that she was taking unfair advantage of her friendship with Dominique and could potentially be causing her trouble. "Wait. Don't answer that. Unless, that is, you want to?"

Dominique laughed. "Let me see how I can phrase

this." Wally had an image of her, eyes closed, trying to find the right words to convey the message without violating police policy. "Okay," said Dominique. "We have not found conclusive evidence at either the theater or the residence or place of business of our suspect." She said those words as if she were making a statement for the media. "However, there is a period that was unaccounted for, when she said she was working on an order but had no receipts for delivery or the name of the customer, and we have learned that Fergie had a falling out with Wade." But then she sighed loudly. "An eye-witness would be really useful," she said wishfully. "But I'm not holding my breath."

Wally' was relieved on behalf of Fergie and her family. On the other hand, Wally well knew that without a real suspect and conviction, Fergie's name might never be cleared. It had been an awful feeling when Nate was under suspicion, and she knew it would be terrible for Fergie and her business, as well as for Belle.

A face popped into Wally's head along with a thought. "Don't give up. There may still be someone who saw something, but that person might not realize it."

"Do you have anyone in mind?"

"I'd rather not say. I'll get back to you."

"Wally, you can't go questioning people. That's for the police to do."

"Have you gotten your witness?"

"No."

"Have you questioned everyone?"

"Apparently not the right person. Who are you going to talk to?"

"I'm not ready to talk to that person yet. I am going to try to see the Grangers first. But I don't think I'm going to do the talking alone," said Wally, as her strategy started falling into place. "I think I'm going to have Tillie go with me. She has a better relationship with them, from the time they spent together after the murder. Don't worry, they aren't suspects. Just potential leads."

"Just be careful," Dominique said. "And call me as soon as you have something."

"You'll be the first person I call."

Wally pulled out her cell phone as she went upstairs to get ready and speed dialed Tillie, keeping her greetings and catching up short so she could get right to the point. "I need to talk to the Grangers."

"Are you still investigating the murder?"

"I'm not investigating," Wally protested. "I'm just tying up loose ends. Dominique will find out who really killed Wade."

"Martha and Belle will be so relieved. They don't believe Fergie did it."

"How did--?"

"Martha called me," Tillie said cheerfully. "She wanted me to talk you into investigating. I told her that she should call you. I knew you wouldn't turn her down."

"I couldn't. I still feel guilty for the police looking at Fergie in the first place. That's why I want to talk to the Grangers. Since they produced the play, I thought maybe they would know something."

"Ooh, do you think one of them did it?

"No. Not at all." Wally began to wonder if she was making a mistake.

"Okay," said Tillie, "so how can I help?"

"I thought that since you know them, maybe you might help me ask about people who might have been affecting things behind the scenes as the production progressed. They may know of people whom Wade might have dealt with that no one really knows about."

"Do you want me to call them right now?"

Wally glanced at the clock. "We'll have to hurry. I have to have dinner on the table by six, you know."

"Piece of cake. As long as they're home. I'll call you

right back."

The dough would have to rise again for another hour, so theoretically there was time to get a few more answers before the holiday started. It was crazy, of course, to even attempt it, but Wally couldn't let it wait until after the holiday, three days from now. She knew how awful it felt to have suspicion hanging over the head of someone she loved and she didn't want to cause Martha or Belle any more grief.

The phone rang. "We're on," said Tillie. "I'll be waiting outside."

Chapter Twenty

Wally drove to Tillie's as quickly as she could, planning her approach when they visited the Grangers. But when she arrived at the senior citizen home her stomach dropped. Standing beside Tillie were none other than Biddy and Orli. As casually as she could, Wally hit the automatic door locks.

Tillie tried opening the door as Wally pulled to a stop in front of her building. Wally hit the lock button again and again, as if she were trying to open the doors and put up her hands as if to say she didn't know what was wrong. Then she lowered the front passenger window just enough so that she could talk quietly without Tillie's friends hearing. Tillie made a face and leaned in.

"Why aren't the doors opening?"

"Gee, I don't know," said Wally. "Maybe because I don't think we need to take four people to go ask a few questions."

"They just want to get a gander at the house. What if they promise not to say a word?"

As if that were possible, Wally thought. She had to stick to her guns. "It's an imposition to arrive with an entourage under these circumstances. The Grangers won't like it."

Tillie waved off Wally's protests. "Oh, sure they would. We all had a good time that night Wade Fuller was killed, once we got over the initial shock. Did you know we had to convince them that they had nothing to do with the murder? They thought it wouldn't have happened if they hadn't produced the play."

Wally could almost understand how the Grangers might have come to that conclusion. "In a way they were right, but only by a technicality. I suspect the person who killed Wade would have found another way if it couldn't be done in the theater."

"That's what we said. Let's go. They've invited all of us for tea."

Wally thought she must have heard wrong. "Why would they do that?"

"I think maybe they're a little lonely," Orli said. "Most of their friends have gone--"

Biddy cut her off. "To Florida."

"I haven't got time for tea," Wally protested.

Tillie smiled. "Let's face it, Wally, you don't have time to be standing here arguing, do you?"

Wally hit the unlock button and started doing some deep breathing exercises while the three women got themselves settled in the car. Tillie, as usual, put the shoulder harness of the seat belt under her arm, which set off similar actions by the women in the back seat. They all discussed what a great idea that was on the way to the Grangers' house, which stood at the top of the hill overlooking New York City.

A maid answered the door of the white columned Georgian house, the kind that had been bought with old money and kept up with new wealth. It had belonged to Nanette's family but she and Darby, who had made his own fortune developing an office temp school and agency, had not moved in until Nanette's mother was gone. Over the years, the couple had become the cream of Grosvenor society.

Wally and Tillie were invited inside but they had to wait for Orli and Biddy who were walking up the slate path admiring the flowers and shrubs. Wally felt as if she could easily jump out of her skin.

Finally they were all there and they were led into the solarium. The glass room stood next to the pool and Tillie's friends barely said more than a quick hello to their hosts before going to stand at the glass and ogle the backyard.

"Your home is lovely," said Tillie.

"Thanks for letting us come," Wally added.

"Sit and have some tea," Nanette said, looking up as her maid brought in a heavy looking tray. Wally was surprised, delighted and appalled to see that it was going to be a rather large tea, since there were scones, berries, and clotted cream. Her stomach jumped for joy while her brain silently shouted that there was no time. Naturally politeness and no lunch won out and Wally helped herself.

When she could talk, though, Wally explained why they had come. She watched as the other ladies took small pieces of scones and sipped tea and hoped they would keep quiet. "I wanted to talk about the production of the play. Were there any people who were involved before the play was moved to the new theater who were no longer involved afterward?"

"No. Except for the church theater's porter," said Nanette. She was wearing a long, printed caftan with a high neck. She had on a string of large pearls and rings on each of her somewhat knobby but well manicured fingers. Her golden coif was flawlessly swept into a French twist.

"I offered to pay his salary and find him a place in the production, so he wouldn't lose out," Darby added. His sport jacket and bow tie with matching pocket square and perfectly polished shoes made him the picture of refinement as he sat rigidly erect buttering a scone.

"Who was that?" Wally asked. "I don't remember him."

"He didn't take my offer. He thanked me, though, but he wanted to look after the repairs."

"I know there were several people who were new to the production when it moved to the new theater," Wally said. "Did you come to know any of them?"

"Yes," said Nanette. She seemed profoundly sad. "Harvey Floyd, the theater manager. He was so helpful and so warm and welcoming. He was there the first thing in the morning, and he was always available for deliveries, even late at night."

"That's true," Darby put in. "One night during rehearsals he went back to the theater when I told him I'd left my reading glasses, then he brought them here. It could have waited until morning, but he said it was no trouble. He was the opposite of that Fuller boy."

Wally had to stop a minute at the thought of someone calling Wade a boy. It made sense, however, as he had grown up in Grosvenor and the Grangers had lived here their whole married lives. And it could also explain why Harvey was at the theater that late at night. He was either working or someone had called him there, saying there was a problem. Wally hoped there was something she could do to find out who that was, after she cleared Fergie. "What did Wade do to you?"

"He tried to ridicule me," said Darby. "It doesn't matter."

Nanette shook her head. "But he was so rude." She turned to Wally. "I'll tell you what he did," said Nanette.

Darby shook his head. "No, darling, it wasn't important."

"Yes it was. And cruel."

"Please tell us," said Tillie, who was staring at Wally with a little smile on her lips. Wally could only shrug.

Nanette turned to face Tillie. "I don't know if you are aware of this, but Xancie Valent is a pseudonym for my Darby. He wrote the play."

Every face in the room turned to look at Darby, some with open mouths. It wasn't a pretty sight.

Wally recovered first. "It's a wonderful play," she said, thinking she couldn't wait to tell this to Louise. "How did you ever think of that clever plot and all the twists?"

Darby, whose face had turned red, looked at Nanette who was laughing. "Darby was only writing about how we met. Many of those things really happened."

"Oh, I exaggerated it all," said Darby. "Your mother was not the ogre I portrayed."

"So you were the diner owner's son?" Orli asked.

"If you'll think back to the rehearsals," Biddy said impatiently, "the girl did not end up with the young man she was with in the beginning. She ended up with her mother's secretary. I thought you said you understood the play."

Orli looked confused, but Darby patted her hand. "I know. It was confusing. I was Nanette's mother's secretary, and I was in love with Nanette. She was in love with me, but we both knew that her mother would not allow her to marry a man in my circumstances. So we concocted, with the help of a few of our friends, this scheme to make Nanette's mother think she had fallen in love with the son of a diner owner. The story lent itself perfectly to the type of farce I wrote."

Two short acts later, Wally thought. And it would explain why no one had ever heard of Xancie Valent. "So you decided to produce it yourself at the church theater, since it was so close to your heart?" she asked.

Darby nodded happily. "You have that a bit backwards. I usually give the theater group a big donation to help with the annual play, but times were rough this year for so many people and donations to cover all the other expenses were down. They weren't going to be able to produce a show at all because they couldn't afford the licensing fees on top of everything else. I didn't want to see them cancelling the show, so I wrote them a check for the whole thing, and gave them my script to use however they wanted."

"But you said that Wade gave you a hard time."

"He really didn't want us to perform the play in "his" new theater. He threatened to expose me as the playwright, which, as you can imagine, might have been embarrassing if the play bombed."

"Was that the only reason he didn't want you to do the play?" Wally asked. "Because the theater hadn't yet opened and is being geared for professional performances?"

Nanette had a small smile on her lips, as if she had a pleasant secret. She walked over to where he sat on the couch and perched on its arm. "Tell them, Darby."

The old man chuckled. "Did you ever see the whole play?"

Wally, Tillie, Orli and Biddy all shook their heads. "Just bits and pieces," Wally told him.

"Well, if you had, you might have seen that the character played by Doug Norton, that of the young man's father and restaurant owner, was somewhat like Wade Fuller—brash, arrogant, and a know-it-all. I'm not sure that anyone would necessarily recognize him, but I guess if one thinks everything is about himself, he could feel embarrassment."

"I wouldn't have thought he could ever feel embarrassed, dear," Nanette said. She put her arm around her husband and he reached his age-mottled hand up for hers. Wally hoped she and Nate would still be that close when they got to be the age of the Grangers.

The gesture had not been lost on Tillie and her gang. Wally felt a pang of sadness for the three widows who were all around the same mid-eighties age. "Did Wade ever see that scene being rehearsed?"

"I believe he did," said Nanette. "I remember studiously avoiding his gaze. But Darby looked him right in the eye." She turned to her husband. "You can be a bit arrogant yourself," she chided.

"Did anyone else know you modeled Doug's character on Wade Fuller?" Wally asked.

"I know Doug did. He knew I had written the play and he came to me to see if I could give him some more insight into the character. I said, 'In the first act, just pretend you're Wade Fuller.' And he said, 'In other words, Fuller of it.' We both got a good laugh out of that one."

Wally loved word play just as much as anyone but this whole conversation, interesting as it might be, was not getting them anywhere. "Did you see anyone who had a grudge against Wade?"

"Everyone from Harvey Floyd to Teri, the young woman in the ticket booth, rolled their eyes when they saw him coming. I don't think there were too many people who liked seeing Wade walk through the theater doors."

Tillie and her friends nodded knowingly at each other.

"Harvey Floyd had a problem with Wade?"

"Harvey was the champion of our little production," Darby said. "Over and over he assured Wade that there wouldn't be a problem. And there wouldn't have been, not if Wade hadn't been murdered."

"It's ironic, actually," Nanette said.

"This was just wonderful," Wally said by way of explaining why she was getting ready to leave. "But we have to be going. Thanks so much for your hospitality and for answering our questions."

Tillie held her tongue until they were out on the curb. "That was great," she said. "We found out so many things."

"Nothing that will help to clear you-know-who."

"Who?" asked Orli. Biddy looked at Tillie and they exchanged winks.

"No one," Tillie said. "Wally is just doing her job, looking for a suspect."

"It's not my job," Wally said. "My job is to get home

211

and get dinner on the table. It's getting late so could we please hurry? Everyone will be arriving soon."

As soon as she dropped off Orli and Biddy, Wally went home, taking Tillie with her. "That little outing cost me some time," she mumbled, feeling frustrated.

Tillie adjusted her seat belt, only adding to Wally's exasperation. "Did you say something, dear?"

After a deep breath, slowly expelled, Wally plastered a smile on her face. "Are you up for helping out tonight?"

"Absolutely."

Wally assigned Tillie the job of setting the table while she punched down the dough and shaped it, covering the two coiled loaves with dish towels to keep them moist. There was at least an hour left of rising for the dough so Wally decided to run into town for the last few ingredients on her list, leaving Tillie to keep an eye on things, knowing they'd be in good hands.

Ever since the new upscale grocery store had opened the town was more crowded with people coming to buy delicacies not usually available nearby. It took Wally a while to find a parking space and she ended up parking across from Marcella's. She shook her head. Could she never get a rest from thinking about Wade's death?

She walked the two blocks back to the store, which was downhill, meaning she would have to carry her groceries back up to her car. Once inside, Wally found the store bustling with so many delicious smells and inviting fruits, vegetables, and cheeses, that she ended up with two grocery bags plus her usual canvas tote. Walking back up the hill to her car with the lowering western sun in her eyes was a slow drudge.

A figure was silhouetted ahead of her and Wally recognized Rolly, standing right on the curb looking like he was going to cross. Some drivers slowed to let him go across, but when he stayed where he was, they were immediately honked by drivers in the cars behind them.

Grove Street was a major east west artery in the county and it was rush hour. Cars streamed down the hill and after going around the curve, merged into the one lane which fed into the town center. Patience was thin, and if Rolly wasn't going to cross, he would have to move away from the curb to avoid causing an accident.

A warning light two tenths of a mile up the hill, before the curve, indicated an upcoming red light, which was helpful since it was impossible to see what was ahead. Even so, a red light just before the merge usually came as a surprise. Drivers squeezed their vehicles into the painted warning area, trying to get past each other and into a better position. Visibility was limited. What Rolly was doing was dangerous.

Wally hadn't seen Rolly in while, but it was clear that he was in one of his bad moods. She went over to talk to him and hopefully draw him into a safer place. "Hi, Rolly, how are you?"

He shook his head, furrowing his brow, but didn't speak.

"Are you trying to cross the street?"

"Can't get away," he mumbled, or at least that was how it sounded.

He seemed so agitated Wally wondered if she should call someone to help him. She could call over to Telly's and if Stacey was there she could come and take Rolly home.

Wally put her bags down and reached into her purse for her cell phone, only to remember she had taken it out to call Tillie earlier. It was probably still on her dresser where she had left it. So she tried to think of where she might be able to make a call, since there was no public phone on the street.

The dance school was closed, Wally discovered, so she ran into Fergie's flower shop right next to the school. The door was open but Wally found the shop empty. She hurried through to the back room, figuring to find Fergie there, but there was no one.

The rear door was open so Wally went outside. There was still no sign of Fergie, but her aunt's car and her delivery van, painted on the sides with Blossoms' flowery logo, were there in the rutted and muddy parking lot. The van's rear door open. Wally went over to it.

Two gorgeous arrangements wrapped in cellophane stood in back. Obviously Fergie was getting on with her business. Wally had to give her credit. It must be hard working while worrying about being under suspicion, no matter how erroneous.

She didn't have time, though, to wait to talk to Fergie. For all she knew, Rolly could be getting into an accident at any minute. Leaning on the side of the van to help her squeeze between the two vehicles, she went around it to go back to the street, Wally noticed something she hadn't known before. The sign on the van wasn't painted on. It was on top of something. On a whim, Wally poked her finger nail at the side of the sign and discovered it was a giant rubberized magnet that could be removed. That was probably a good idea for resale, Wally thought, just as the next idea crowded the first one out and she gasped.

It was also a way to disguise the car. Without the sign, the van could pass for the one that almost hit Martha and Belle. And Wade.

"What are you doing?" said a shrill voice.

Wally turned to face Fergie, who looked angrier than Wally had ever seen anyone. "Did you see Rolly outside?" Wally asked. "He's in trouble and I came to use your phone to call for help."

"I'm sure Rolly is fine," Fergie said. "He knows how to take care of himself."

"He's too near the traffic," Wally insisted.

"What is he, five? He's a big boy." Fergie shook her head. "Not everyone is in nursery school, you know. Now,

I asked you a question. What are you doing with my van?"

Wally tried to think what the best approach would be for handling Fergie. She tried innocence, although she had little hope of it working. The facts were too obvious, but while she was thinking of her next tack, she gave it a try. "What do you mean?"

Fergie gave her a look that told her Wally she was no idiot. "You know about my van. What else do you think you know?"

"I don't think you meant to hurt your Aunt Martha in the parking lot that afternoon," Wally said as reasonably as she could. "It was just an accident. They were in the wrong place at the wrong time."

Fergie frowned. "I thought they'd left already. All I could see was Wade."

"We don't have to tell the police," Wally said, trying to calm her. "Then your mother won't find out."

Fergie looked at Wally as if she were weighing Wally's words. An awkward moment passed before Fergie said, "We should go help Rolly."

With relief, Wally hurried ahead of Fergie to the street. Rolly was still there, standing near the curb, next to Wally's groceries. He turned when Wally called out to him and started toward her, but then his eyes widened and he got even more agitated. "What are you doing?" he asked Fergie.

Suddenly Wally felt Fergie crowding her toward Rolly and the curb. The light up the street had just changed. As the cars picked up speed coming down the hill, they were way too close to Wally. She could feel not only the wind as they went by, but also the heat from their exhausts. They wouldn't be able to stop if someone was accidentally pushed out into the street.

Wally was afraid that was exactly what Fergie had in mind.

Rolly was talking. At first Wally couldn't make out

what he was saying. "No more, not again."

Fergie turned toward him. "What did you say?"

Rolly looked at her. "I can't love you anymore."

"You've loved me since seventh grade," Fergie said. "You can't stop now."

"Not anymore. You do terrible things."

Wally took the opportunity to wiggle out from between the two of them and away from the curb. But her fear didn't diminish because Rolly and Fergie, now aware of only themselves and arguing loudly, were still dangerously close to the traffic.

Wally ran up the hill and started waving her hands. Traffic stopped and she pointed at the quarrelling couple to get the drivers to understand the danger. "Call the police," she said to someone who had lowered his window.

Fergie seemed to become aware of the stopped traffic and ran away in the direction of her store. A moment later her van tore out of the driveway and went down the side street.

Rolly stood staring after her as Wally came to guide him away from the curb. "They are going to make me go back there again," he said. Wally figured he meant the hospital.

"Maybe not. Before the police get here, tell me one thing. Have you been upset because of something you saw Fergie do?"

"I loved her."

"But she disappointed you, didn't she?"

"She did bad things."

As much as she wanted to hear more, Wally didn't dare ask another question because she wanted Rolly's statement to be fresh and untainted by something she said. "Everything will be okay, Rolly. You'll see."

#

Wally looked flushed when Dominique and Ryan pulled up into the driveway of Blossoms. They had

216

received the call about the incident on Grove but were advised to turn at the first street after the shop and go to the driveway. There was concern about accidents being caused by commuters driving past the scene of the investigation.

"What happened?" Dominique asked her friend.

Wally took her aside and spoke softly. "It doesn't matter. What does is that Rolly Sherman knows something about who nearly hit Martha. It was Fergie, who removed the signs from the sides of her van. She as much as admitted it to me and I believe Rolly saw it. There is also a chance that he knows who killed Wade."

"Did he tell you all of this?" Ryan asked. "It could compromise--"

"No. I didn't ask him anything. I think he's ready to tell someone what he saw but you should understand that he is quite upset. He had strong feelings for Fergie, that's why he didn't come forward before."

"He was a witness to the murder?" Ryan scowled. "How could that be?"

"I'm not sure but if you think about it, Rolly is always out on the streets, so he probably saw a lot of things most people wouldn't as they rushed from place to place. In addition, he had a crush on Fergie and stayed close. He also started acting strangely soon after the car accident."

"He should have come forward," Ryan said.

Wally turned to Dominique. "I want to go with Rolly to the police station. Could I just borrow one of your cell phones, first?"

Dominique handed over her phone and Wally used it to call Nate. "Please paint on the egg wash and stick the challot in the oven. I'll explain later."

When Wally gave the phone back Dominique put her hand onto Wally's. "I know that your New Year holiday is starting tonight and I know it is important for your family that you be there. Don't you need to get home?"

"I have a little more time. I want to hear what Rolly has to say."

"You won't be able to sit in on the questioning," Ryan pointed out.

Dominique sighed. "Go home, Wally. We'll take care of this. I'll tell you what I can when I can."

Wally looked at her and smiled. "Thanks. You're right. I'll go." She went over to Rolly who was looking frightened, confused, and as though he'd lost his best friend. "Everything will work out. I'll check on you soon."

Although she knew she should go straight home, Wally made one more stop at Telly's. Stacey was grateful for the news, especially after Telly let her have the rest of the night off to go take care of her friend. Wally knew Rolly would be well looked after.

Chapter Twenty-one

"Is it all over?" Wally asked Dominique after the holiday. It was Saturday evening, and Wally had called her as soon as she had a chance.

"You missed a lot," Dominique said.

"Did you find Fergie?"

"Yes. She didn't get very far. She was driving her aunt's car and we put out a bulletin on it."

"Did she confess?"

"No. But we feel we have a good case against her. Rolly has been talking to us and he seems to have observed a lot of Fergie's activities. He also said he knows where she buried some of the evidence and we are going to look for it."

"Where?"

"What do you mean, where? We can handle this."

"I'm sure you can. But I want to see with my own eyes the evidence that clears Nate for good."

Dominique sighed. "It's in her mother's yard."

"I'll be right over."

"Please don't tell anyone about this," Dominique said.

"I won't, I promise."

Wally wasted no time. "I'll be back," she told Nate, who was in their kitchen, catching up on the mail.

He looked up, a question forming.

"I'll explain later." She grabbed her keys and left.

Wally drove in record time over to Belle Schulz's house in one of the oldest sections of town. When she got

219

there she found several police cars, along with some of the big klieg lights used by news crews to have "live coverage" at eleven in front of closed businesses. Wally groaned. She wasn't ready for the local news teams to descend on the town. Luckily, the lights seemed to belong to the Grosvenor department of public works, and they were aimed at the flower beds. Two photographers had their cameras aimed at the area being excavated and they were clearly documenting the whole project.

Rolly stood, head down, nearby. He looked up when Wally approached, then hung his head again. "I'm sorry," he said.

"It wasn't your fault, Rolly," Wally said. "You didn't do anything."

"I should have told the police what I knew. Maybe all of this wouldn't have happened."

Wally let him talk. She agreed with him, he should have spoken up. But she wanted to hear what he had to say.

"I loved her once," he whispered. "I didn't want her to be like that."

There was not much to say to Rolly in the way of comforting words. Wally turned her attention to the officers with shovels, who were digging up a flower bed full of yellow mums. It took only a short time and then a black plastic garbage bag was pulled out of the earth.

It was immediately transferred to a car bearing the insignia of the Essex County Sheriff's office and driven away. There was a bit more digging, but then the search was ended.

"I can't believe you didn't open the bag," Wally said to Dominique. "For all you know it didn't contain any evidence at all."

"We can't take the chance of contaminating it," Ryan explained. "I'm sorry, Mrs. Morris."

He seemed sincere. Maybe she had finally won over

Dominique's partner. It was a little consolation.

"I think I'll be going now," Wally said. "If you could just let me know what you found?"

Dominique smiled, not very convincingly. "I'll see what I can do."

\#

"So what did you learn?" Nate asked, when Wally returned home. He was still in the kitchen, reading the local newspaper with its week old news. Wally suspected there were references to the allegations against Nate, since he hadn't been cleared until after the newspaper went to press.

She looked forward to the restoration of her husband's good name. "They found some evidence in a plastic bag in Belle's yard. I think it should prove Fergie did it." Wally still felt horrible that the florist had turned out to be the murderer, but she was over the guilt of having pointed the finger in Fergie's direction. Still, she couldn't imagine how poor Belle and Martha were coping.

Nate frowned at the newspaper, folded it, and looked up at his wife. "What was in it?"

"I don't know."

"So you wasted a trip?"

"It's not a waste if it's more evidence that you are an innocent man."

He raised his eyebrows. "So you think I'm completely innocent, huh?" He stood, pulling Wally close, and began to nuzzle her neck. She reached her arms around him and-- the phone rang.

"Let it ring," Nate said.

"I would," Wally said, disengaging from Nate's embrace, "but it could be Dominique." She picked up the phone.

"I have the best news!" Louise cried, nearly deafening Wally in the process. She had to hold the phone away from her head, which gave Nate a chance to listen in.

221

"What is it?" Wally asked.

"You aren't going to believe it. I mean, I can't believe it and I already know it. And it just gets better and better."

Nate grabbed Wally's hand with the phone and spoke into the mouthpiece. "Tell us already."

"I'm not sure how it happened," Louise chortled, "but I got a call tonight from none other than Lance Palmer himself. He said they are going to do the play, for one night only, and he wants me to be the star. He said without me he isn't going to take the time to do it."

Wally could well imagine how special Louise was feeling. "That's great! When will it be?"

"The theater has an opening in four weeks. They are going to hold the postponed opening night ceremonies after the play. Aren't you excited?"

"We are."

"Nate, you'd better promise not to budge out of your seat that night. We don't want any repeats of the last time."

Nate held up his hand, even though Louise wouldn't see it. "I promise."

"I can't stay on the phone talking to you," Louise said, as if she had just realized something momentous. "I have to go over my lines. Talk to you soon. Oh, I hope I'm not just dreaming."

Wally had no chance to say good-bye. Louise had hung up. Wally put the phone back on the hook, but it immediately rang again. This time it was Dominique. Wally didn't even bother to say hello, before she said, "What did you find?"

"A bloody raincoat, gloves and other items, including a baseball cap and a roll of duct tape that I suspect might also have Nate's fingerprints on it."

"But it was stolen from Nate's car! You aren't going to go back to thinking he had anything to do with it, are you?"

"I don't think so," Dominique said. "It does shed

some light on how Ms. Schulz committed the murder. Rolly Sherman gave us an eye-witness account, saying he saw Ms. Schulz wearing the cap and bloody raincoat coming out of the back of the theater. He says he saw her throw the knife in the dumpster before going to the back of her shop, which explains some of the rest of our questions. He said she was wearing gloves, which is why there were no fingerprints other than Nate's on the knife.

"Mr. Sherman also explained that he saw Ms. Schulz drive into her shop's driveway just after the accident occurred across the street where her aunt and her mother were nearly hit, and he said he saw her replace the magnetic signs on the side of the van. He was the one to tell her that her aunt had been hurt. By her reaction, saying she didn't mean it, he knew she had been the one driving and what she had intended."

Wally thought back to when she went to the scene of Martha and Belle's accident in the driveway of Wade's restaurant. Fergie arrived right afterward with a first-aid kit. Wally had thought Fergie must have gotten there immediately after the accident, and had assumed that she then went back to her shop for supplies after seeing that her mother and aunt were bleeding. But if she hadn't, if she had only known to bring a first-aid kit because Rolly told her that her mother was hurt, then her appearance at the scene was her first. Why? Because she had been the one driving the van that caused the accident?

Wally had a chill, knowing that if she had that information, that it was Fergie's first appearance on the scene, she would have wondered what took Fergie so long to get there after the accident. If she had asked that question, maybe Fergie could have been put away before she committed murder. If, if.

Dominique continued. "Mr. Sherman had also been the recipient of Ms. Schulz's displaced ire after Wade broke up with her. And he knew she was very upset earlier on the day of the parking lot incident when she lost the two huge flower orders because of Wade."

"He knew so much."

"There may be more. Mr. Sherman placed Ms. Schulz in the alley of the theater on the night of the fire. It was much earlier in the evening, and when she saw him, she left."

"Yet he said nothing."

"Not a word," Dominique said. "He must have loved her very much."

Wally agreed. "I wonder if his having seen Fergie act in that way was what caused Rolly to get so agitated again."

"He has been much calmer since he told us what he knew," Dominique said. "I'm hoping he will be okay now. That will surely help our case, when he has to testify."

"Good," Wally said. "That woman needs to stay somewhere where the rest of us will be safe."

"One last thing," Dominique said. "Preliminary results show the blood on the raincoat matched Wade Fuller's. I'll talk to you soon."

Wally stared at the phone for a moment. She still had questions, but maybe they could wait. Her husband needed some attention. She hung up the phone. It immediately rang again. This time it was Norman.

"She wasn't just dreaming," he said. "Harvey Floyd woke up from his coma on Thursday morning. He can't remember very much, and he thinks the play is still a few days away. When the Grangers heard that, they set some wheels in motion to make it happen."

"I didn't want to say this to Louise," Wally said, "but what about the rest of the cast? Wasn't Doug Norton going out of town? And the Clarks were fighting. Will they still do it?"

"Yes. It was all being arranged before Lance called Louise. He wasn't going to risk disappointing her."

Norman paused, but Wally had the sense he had more to say. She was right. "He isn't such a bad guy," Norman admitted. "And his behavior wasn't as creepy as I first thought. When we were in the emergency room he told me that Louise reminds him of his favorite aunt."

If so much hadn't been going on at the time, Wally would have thought it was cute that Norman was jealous of Lance's attention to Louise. A husband needed to feel his wife still had allure for other men. On the other hand, it was good he had an adequate explanation.

"Go help Louise with her lines," Wally said. Then she hung up the phone, willing it not to ring again.

#

There was an air of excitement not felt the first time around as the opening/closing performance of *Anyone Else* was ready to start. The theater was standing room only and Tillie, Orli, and Biddy were in place prepared to sell their snacks, although this time they were inside the large lobby of the new GrovePAC.

New programs had been printed to replace the originals. The notable modification to the original cast, Louise Fisch, who had gone from understudy to leading lady, had been floating for weeks in happy anticipation.

"You have to focus," Wally told her friend. "You don't want to make mistakes."

"I'll be okay," she promised. "It's so good to have everyone back. With the exception of Courtney Haven, of course." She smiled at herself in the dressing room mirror. "Doesn't everyone look great?"

Wally agreed. All the younger actors had returned and were excited to be there. The Clarks, the one married couple in the show, had apparently reconciled and Doug Norton had postponed his trip out of town. Lance had persuaded the possible backers of his new show to come see the play and everyone in the cast planned to do what they could to help their director's career.

The audience was also comprised of several members of the news media who had descended on Grosvenor when the murder occurred and had returned once Martha Ferguson Shultz, Fergie, was arraigned. B. J. Waters was there along with her camera man. No doubt she would be standing in front of the empty new theater at eleven, wrapping up the story of the murder in Grosvenor, New Jersey.

The cast and crew had some good news on the day of the performance. Harvey Floyd, the stage manager, was being released from the hospital and would be in the audience. He still had no idea what had happened on the night of the fire. Wally thought maybe that was a good thing.

"They're here," said Babbette. Wally looked out into the audience and saw the Grangers, Darby resplendent in black tie and Nanette exquisite in a glittering evening gown, entering the theater. Since the news came out that Mr. Granger was the playwright, they had been receiving congratulations from as far away as San Francisco. In fact, Lance was in negotiations for a possible future production of the play off Broadway.

Nate and Norman were taking their places in the audience. Wally hoped that no matter what, Nate wouldn't budge. At least she knew he wasn't going to be chasing after Fred Neimeyer tonight.

It took some persuasion, but Nate had finally explained that Fred hadn't believed that Wade would destroy the incriminating documentation of his co-mingling of client funds after he got the money he needed for the liquor license. On the evening of the play opening, Fred planned to break into his office to retrieve it. Nate had figured that out and went to make sure he didn't. That was when Alberto saw him behind the restaurant.

Luckily, Wanda was the one who had the evidence of Fred's misused client trust account. Otherwise the police

226

would have found it during the investigation. It was all for the best. Wanda would have lost her stake in the restaurant and her hold over Fred if the truth came out, so she gave it back to him. Wally was still annoyed at Nate for putting himself in the middle of the whole thing, but she understood.

Louise's performance was brilliant. What she lacked in experience she more than made up in emotion. Her comedic timing was remarkable. There was a standing ovation for her at the end of the show and she was presented with the largest bouquet of roses that Wally had ever seen, courtesy of Lance Palmer. Norman's and the Morrises's paled by comparison.

The new star had to "endure" endless interviews by the local media and was also the subject of a segment on New Jersey Network. Norman used his smart phone to set their television to record the news later, to capture Louise's moment in the spotlight.

Since Fred was now a part owner of the restaurant, due to Marcella's and Wanda's need to keep their part in the shakedown quiet, Fred was feeling somewhat generous. He invited the whole cast and crew over to celebrate after the show. Wally and Nate were also invited, so they ditched the GrovePAC opening night gala and went to Marcella's. Wally hoped her daughters and their husbands wouldn't notice.

There was quite a lot to celebrate. Besides Louise's dazzling performance, the play was a triumph. The new president of the GrovePAC board, Norman Fisch, predicted that with all the publicity they generated that night, the theater would be a success.

There were several after-dinner speeches. Lance thanked the cast, with special recognition of his new "diva." Louise thanked everyone, absolutely everyone. At the end of her speech, Fred Neimeyer presented the Morrises with an expensive bottle of Asti. Marcella Fuller

227

added two flutes and a grateful smile.

A little while later, when no one was looking, Nate and Wally, holding hands, picked up their gifts, and disappeared into the cool October evening.

The end

www.ingramcontent.com/pod-product-compliance
Lightning Source LLC
Chambersburg PA
CBHW070106260626
47160CB00004B/1340